GREAT HORSE STORIES

Compiled by Suzanne LeVert
Illustrations by John Speirs

Julian Messner  New York

Published by JULIAN MESSNER, a division of Simon & Schuster, Inc.,
Simon & Schuster Building
1230 Avenue of the Americas
New York, New York 10020

Designed by Gill Speirs
Manufactured in the United States of America
10 9 8 7 6 5 4 3 2 1
JULIAN MESSNER and colophon are trademarks
of Simon & Schuster, Inc.
Also available in Little Simon trade edition.

Library of Congress Cataloging in Publication Data

Great Horse Stories

    Contents: The lonely beach / by Helen Griffiths—
Midnight / by Will James—The winning of Dark Boy / by
Josephine Noyes Felts—[etc.]
    1. Horses—Juvenile fiction. 2. Children's stories,
American. 3. Children's stories, English. [1. Horses—
Fiction. 2. Short stories] I. LeVert, Suzanne.
II. Speirs, John, ill. III. Title: Great Horse Stories
IV. Title: Book of horse stories.
PZ10.3.S396117 1984   [Fic]   84-14370
ISBN 0-671-52591-3
ISBN 0-671-53132-8 (Lib. Ed.)

DATE DUE

JUL 15 1987			
AUG 03 1987			
NOV 2 - 1987			
SEP 9 1988			
JUL 2 7 1996			

GREAT HORSE STORIES

ACKNOWLEDGEMENTS

Peter Zachary Cohen, Chapters 1, 2, 8 & 17 from MORENA. Copyright © 1970 Peter Zachary Cohen. Reprinted with the permission of Atheneum Publishers.

"Spurs for Antonia" by K.W. Eyres. Reprinted with permission from the book SPURS FOR ANTONIA, copyright 1943. Published by David McKay Company, Inc.

"The Winning of Dark Boy" by Josephine Noyes Felt, originally published in CALLING ALL GIRLS magazine, 1945. Reprinted with the permission of Parent's Magazine Enterprises.

Will James, "Midnight" in SUN UP. Copyright 1931 Charles Scribner's Sons. Copyright renewed 1959 Auguste Dufault. Reprinted with the permission of Charles Scribner's Sons.

"The Lonely Beach" from STALLION OF THE SANDS by Helen Griffiths. Reprinted by permission of the author. Copyright 1968 by Helen Griffiths.

Lynn Hall, Chapter I from DANZA!. Copyright © 1981 Lynn Hall. Reprinted with the permission of Charles Scribner's Sons.

"The Gift" from THE LONG VALLEY by John Steinbeck. Copyright 1933 renewed © 1961 by John Steinbeck. Reprinted by permission of Viking Penguin Inc.

CONTENTS

FOREWORD

I will not change my horse with any that treads . . . When I bestride him, I soar, I am a hawk. He trots the air. The earth sings when he touches it. The basest horn of his hoof is more musical than the pipe of Hermes . . . He's the color of nutmeg and of the heat of the ginger . . . He is pure air and fire, and the dull elements of earth and water never appear in him, but only in patient stillness while his rider mounts him . . . It is the prince of palfreys. His neigh is like the bidding of a monarch, and his countenance enforces homage.

William Shakespeare, King Henry V, *Act III, Scene 7*

What could match the thrill and joy of being atop your very own horse, controlling his every move, yet flying as free as the wind as you gallop away? Some of the young men and women you'll meet in this collection have been lucky enough to experience that exhilarating adventure, and many of you, I'm sure, are dreaming about it right this very minute.

From the earliest days of man's history, the horse has been his constant companion and partner—in everything from fast-paced racing to gory battles in war, from quiet rides through the woods to perilous stagecoach travel through the American West. As William Shakespeare so eloquently expresses above, man has been awed by the power and grace of this magnificent beast.

American culture is especially rich with legends and traditions surrounding man and his relationship to the horse. We're all familiar with the lonesome cowboy and his trusted, sometimes only, friend along the hot, dusty trail; the Pony Express man, depending on the speed and stamina of his horse to reach his post safely, with mail for the Old West's pioneers or with urgent messages about the Indian wars and approaching danger; the dignified Civl War general, commanding his troops from atop a mighty stallion; the Midwestern farmer, plowing miles of farmland with the help of his faithful workhorse.

But the horse has remained an independent creature, too. Many legends exist about wild ponies in the hills of Montana, fierce white stallions who refuse to be captured, or independent colts unable to be broken and tamed. The sight of a horse roaming with his herd, galloping across the plain, so powerful in his freedom, beckons to that free spirit in us all and reminds us of the deep mysteries of nature.

In the ten stories chosen for this collection, these and other images of the mighty horse are brought to life. In Will James's "Midnight," written in a nitty-gritty cowboy slang, a man who has spent much of his life capturing wild stallions to sell and tame is himself caught by the beauty and strength of one special horse, and concedes that some things are meant to stay wild and free. An altogether different side of that coin can be found in "The Winning of Dark Boy," an exciting adventure by Josephine Noyes Felts. Here, an untamed and dangerous horse is broken in when a young girl, desperate to save her friend's family from imminent danger, musters up the courage to mount and ride him—her only chance to find help in time.

A young boy's struggle to survive is portrayed in Paul Zachary Cohen's "Morena," one of three stories in this collection taken from a contemporary novel. The boy, lost and in danger, finds a horse, once abused and forever wary, wandering in the deepening drifts of snow. Their need for each other, and their attempts to understand each other, is tenderly described.

A colorful Western roundup is the setting for a different

x

kind of struggle. Although written in 1943, "Spurs for Antonia" by K. W. Eyres is a rather modern story about an accomplished young horsewoman's successful attempt to be accepted by the male-dominated roundup team.

Two very special stories, one a great American classic and the other a new and equally sensitive tale, concern the powerful facts of life and death. "The Gift," from *The Red Pony,* written by John Steinbeck, is a tender story about a boy's love and devotion to his pony, and his coming to terms with the painful reality of death. "Danza," recently penned by Lynn Hall, explores one boy's wonder and joy at witnessing the birth of a foal.

"Metzengerstein," a supernatural horror story by Edgar Allan Poe, and the charming tale, "The Story of the Enchanted Horse," from *Tales from the Arabian Nights,* are two tales that will make your imagination soar and your spine tingle!

And finally, I have included two stories that are written more from the horse's perspective than the rider's. "Black Beauty," written by Anna Sewell, is a delightful and moving exploration of a horse's life (straight from the horse's mouth!), and "The Lonely Beach," from *Stallions of the Sands* by Helen Griffiths, is a beautifully written tale of a horse's desperate quest for freedom in a world dominated by man.

While choosing this collection, I tried to find the ten stories that would most touch your heart, stimulate your sense of adventure, and be the most fun for you to read. My hope is that these stories fill you with the wonder and love for horses that their authors obviously feel so deeply. Let them take you on a galloping adventure into the fascinating and exciting world of horses!

THE LONELY BEACH

HELEN GRIFFITHS

(from *Stallion of the Sands*)

Once the gauchos had seen the albino stallion and found him so beautiful he knew no peace. There were men who had wanted to forsake the hunt that very day in order to chase after him, and would have done so, but that the one in charge forbade them.

"There's time enough for chasing after fancies when the work is finished," he told them. "When this is done and you've all been paid, then you can chase after a dozen white stallions if you wish."

There were arguments among them, too, about to whom the stallion belonged, for most of them coveted him.

"He's mine. I saw him first," said one.

"But if I catch him first, I shall keep him," another replied. And they squabbled and might even have ended the argument with their knives had not the one who led them been forceful in character and respected by all.

As it was, they held themselves in check until their ox wagons were creaking under the weight of skins and feathers that must be taken to town. They waited until the money had been shared between them, and they passed a few weeks spending it here and there. Then those who were still interested returned to where they had first seen the stallion, and set out in search of him.

Helen Griffiths

By this time, their imaginations had increased the stallion's propensities a hundredfold. He was bigger than any animal they had ever seen, and far more beautiful: swifter than the rushing winter winds, and wilder. They repeated the story so many times that eventually they came to believe it. They convinced themselves and their listeners that the stallion was a horse like no other.

Thus, as spring mellowed into summer, any number of gauchos set out in search of him. Some rode in twos or threes, some rode singly. Some tired of searching for him and were diverted to other things. Others were steadfast, and spent the whole summer crossing and recrossing the district where first they had seen him. Eventually, he was discovered.

There was no mistaking him for another. His pure coloring, his stance, the magnificence of his features were enough to tell any gaucho—even those who had come in search of him only on hearsay—that this was the stallion they sought. But they soon discovered that it would not be easy to catch him.

The albino stallion had become the wariest of creatures now, shunning all company and made fearful by the first hoofbeat that reached his hearing. When the sound of a galloping horse came to his ears, long before it was within his sight he would be away, his ears flattened, his tail held high and streaming out behind him. Rarely did the gauchos see more than this, a fast-fleeing, cloudlike creature, far beyond their reach.

They chased him into the darkness of the nights, and in the mornings they set out in pursuit of him again. With a man behind him, the stallion never faltered. While the gauchos slept, he would still keep running. In the darkest hours before dawn broke, he would pause awhile to draw in deep breaths of air and snatch at the thistles. Then he would be away again, fear stronger than weariness or hunger.

Although the gauchos' horses were fresher than the al-

4

bino, the men lost time searching for his tracks. It might take them half a day to find him. In fast pursuit, the stallion had the advantage, too. He was swifter than the average pony, his legs were much longer, and he carried no weight upon his back.

The summer days lost their freshness and became sullenly hot. Dark clouds gathered at times, but a breeze would come up and push them away. The grass withered, and the ground grew hard. The stallion was weary now, and his pursuers were losing interest. Their first enthusiasm had died long since. Only determination kept them to the chase. But with the burning sun reflecting its heat from the sky and the ground, even determination wavered, and it was difficult to find the albino's tracks on the hard-baked earth.

There came a day when the stallion instinctively knew that no one was following him. He was still cautious; he still kept moving. The whole day passed without sighting a single gaucho. That night he rested and tore at the faded grass with unsatisfied hunger. The next day he was off again. He was more and more certain that no one pursued him. For two or three days, he kept up his flight. It was halfhearted now, and he stopped occasionally to graze. Only when he was finally satisfied that his enemy had left him in peace did he relax.

He grazed and dozed and grazed some more, but always his ears were alert for the slightest unusual sound. A startled bird was all he needed to set him off at a gallop. The days passed by, and nothing happened to disturb his tranquillity. He was thin and jaded, his proud head drooped, but the victory was his. His spirit was as wild as ever.

Because the gauchos had been unable to capture the stallion, they could not forget him. All through the hot summer, when they spent their spare hours exchanging news at the nearest store, or lazed in the shadow of a solitary ombu tree, sipping at the maté pot with friends and circulating stories, the elusive albino was mentioned. He became renowned for his speed and beauty.

Their imagination ever dwelling in the infinite world of spirits and goblins, it did not take the gauchos long to decide that the animal was possessed. In fact, he did not exist at all, but was a demon, appearing only to torment them and lead them to their doom should they insist upon following him. To what strange world would he take them, assuming that he was never lost from sight? Could any gaucho possibly ride him, and what would become of the bold one who tried?

Such were the idle suppositions of the gauchos, haunted by their own loneliness, and populating it with unearthly beings. But even as they wondered thus, it occurred to them that he might just be a horse of flesh and blood, wilier, fleeter, more "gaucho" than their own. They spoke of taking up the chase again, when the cooler weather returned.

So it was that as the summer birds began to grow restless, remembering the warmer northern lands, and the rivers and lakes were no longer graced with glowing flamingo colors, the gauchos were once again foraging the pampa for the albino stallion. Winter had come before they found him. He had wandered a long way southward, almost afraid of the green lands from which sprang so cruel and persistent an enemy. He had gone on and on, until the winds that tickled his nostrils brought only the scent of ice and barrenness. Then he halted. The cold was piercing, and he was not prepared for it.

He found himself among rocks and hard soil and stunted trees, where grass was difficult to discover and unsucculent. At least he found peace there, which was all he sought. His hair grew thicker as the weather worsened. He accustomed himself to the land; to winds that howled and were ever constant; to the nighttime silence—here, the ground was too hard for the vizcachas to burrow. Although he sometimes would lift his head to breathe in the winds that crossed the pampa, bringing with them a reminder of sweet alfalfa and other herbs, he stayed in this new place. There were no men there to molest him.

The days were often gray. As winter deepened, an insidious mist crept over everything, giving strange, unearthly forms to the rocks and bushes. At first, the stallion was disturbed by this strange element that clung so damply to him, and through which he could hardly see at times. The mist had a salty taste. It came in from the great Atlantic, which was not very far away, and it left a tangy flavor on the grass and bushes. There were days when the darkness hardly lifted from the land. Other days, it rained almost constantly. Although the stallion was unused to so harsh a climate, he endured it because of the sanctuary it offered him.

But even there he discovered that his tranquillity was not to last. One day, he heard the shouts of men and the wild galloping of horses' hooves. Now he was truly desperate in his fear, for it seemed that never would he be able to escape them. His lonely sojourn had not caused him to forget their callous ways and their brutality. Again he fled, not knowing where he could go in order to be rid of them forever.

The chase this time was a sporadic one. The gloomy climate protected the stallion in its way, gathering him up in the mist, which was as white as he, and hiding him even from the gauchos' piercing eyes. Seeing him disappear with such rapidity, they were even more convinced that the horse they sought to capture was but a spirit. They, also, were unaccustomed to the sea mists that descended and lifted so rapidly.

"This is a terrain fit for devils," said one, when they had pulled up their mounts in confusion, hardly able to see more than a pace or two on either side. "No wonder that we should find him here."

"Devil or not," replied another, "my three Marias will take care of him."

The "three Marias" referred to the three stone balls of

the bolas. But before they could trip up the stallion they had to be within reach of him, and in the sudden fogs it was difficult to find him. At times, the albino would be hardly more than a mile ahead, stumbling over boulders, almost unable to run. Then, when they thought he was theirs, a blanket of white mist crossed their paths and the stallion disappeared into it.

"It's a devil sent to torment us," insisted the first gaucho again. "I've never chased after any animal so long and still not been able to catch him. He'll lead us to damnation if we insist on following."

And he was all for turning back to a more Christian land, where at least a man could see where he was going. The others had more courage than their companion, and were not afraid of challenging the devil once in a while.

"Let's catch him and give him a good thrashing for our pains," they said. "We'll teach him not to be a devil."

But the days passed. Sometimes they saw him, and sometimes they only heard him. He was never far beyond their reach. Not even the stallion could travel very quickly. He rarely broke from a canter or a hurried trot. The land was rocky and loose with scree, and the mist that hid him from his pursuers also prevented him from making much progress. It seemed to the gauchos that he tormented them on purpose, always within their reach but so elusive. They cursed him and prayed to all the saints for assistance in the capture of him.

The face of the land changed again. Rocky ground gave way to sand. The few bushes and trees were all bent in a westerly direction, deformed by the constant wind. The hills were hills of sand, dunes that constantly altered in height or thickness or position, according to the wind. Desperate was the horse that trod this forsaken countryside, where not even a blade of grass would grow or a bird linger. Brave were the men who followed him, who had never seen such countryside in all their lives, and were convinced that they were pursuing the very devil to his inferno.

Now the wind blew with vengeance, whipping the breath from the stallion's open jaws, almost choking him with its force. His red eyes stung with the salt that clung to the air, his tongue was swollen with thirst. There was a crashing sound in his ears, slow, persistent, eternal—a sound he had never heard before. On he raced, not caring where he went. The gauchos were behind him, and he knew that his energy was failing fast.

That day, a strong wind blew in from the ocean. The mist lifted. The noise that had bewildered the stallion revealed itself as the motion of the sea, huge, gray waves that crashed upon the sand. Now the horse saw that he could go no farther. Ahead of him was the sea, cold, relentless. Behind him were the men.

He halted for a moment, his proud head lifted. The wind caught at the thick forelock and mane, blowing them back from his head and neck. His jaws were wide open, as were his nostrils, as he vainly tried to drag fresh energy into his burning lungs. His eyes seemed to glow in desperation.

It was thus that the gauchos suddenly saw him. They pulled up their horses, hardly able to believe what they saw. Surely there was no horse anywhere as beautiful as this one, who looked almost ready to spring up into the clouds in his effort to escape. Could this be an animal of flesh and blood, so white against the leaden sea, his eyes burning like two fires, his locks like the wings of the angels?

For several moments they hesitated, almost afraid to pursue him farther. Even as they wondered and admired and doubted, the stallion saw them and knew that he was lost. He gave a wild and desperate neigh, which rang above the sound of the crashing waves: he paced along the beach with tossing head, beautiful in his terror.

The gauchos forgot their wonder. They split into two groups, hurriedly making plans. One group galloped to the north, another to the south. On that long and lonely beach the stallion was trapped between them. They came rushing toward him from both directions, the sound of their horses' hooves thundering over the hard sand, which was flung up on every side of them.

The stallion lingered, prancing in small circles, tossing his beautiful head as if in defiance of them. Now he heard the sound of their bolas, cutting viciously through the air. It was a sound that frightened him. He knew what it represented. Within moments his freedom would be lost. They would be upon him.

He made a short run in the direction from which he had come, then changed his course, knowing that it was futile. Back he swirled again. As the gauchos drew near enough to let fly at him with their weapons, the stallion flung himself into the sea, preferring to lose himself among the heavy waters than to surrender to man.

The gauchos saw his whiteness dig deeply into the waves, which were almost black in color, reflecting the gloomy sky. For a second, his mane and tail were banners, flying freely in the wind. Then the water took them, swirling them about his body. The gauchos cried out involuntarily. The horse would be drowned!

They dragged their mounts to a halt at the edge of the sea and watched in silence as the stallion forged his way through the racing waves. Ahead of him was nothing but a wall of mist, behind him an ever-increasing distance be-

tween himself and the shore. The gauchos watched until he disappeared, lost in the sea or the mist, or both. They did not know.

"Well, that's the end of him," remarked one at last, regret in his voice.

The others were silent. Only when they were sure that the horse would not come up out of the waves again, that the adventure was surely ended, as their companion had stated, did they turn their mounts away and return inland.

The beach was lonely again, as ever it had been. When the men and horses had gone, the waves came up over the sand and washed all the hoofprints away.

MIDNIGHT

WILL JAMES

(from *Sun Up*)

Running mustangs had got to be an old game for me; it'd got so that instead of getting some pleasure and excitement out of seeing a wild bunch running smooth into our trap corrals I was finding myself wishing they'd break through the wings and get away.

Now that was no way for a mustang runner to feel but I figgered I just loved horses too well, and thinking it over I was kind of glad I felt that way. I seen that the money I'd get out of the sales of 'em didn't matter so much to me as the liberty I was helping take away from the slick wild studs, mares, and specially the little colts. Yes, sir, it was like getting blood money only worse.

I may be called chicken-hearted and all that but it's my feelings, and them same feelings come from *knowing* horses, and being with 'em steady enough so I near savvy horse language. My first light of day was split by the shape of a horse tied back of the wagon I was born in, and from then on horses was my main interest.

I'd got to be a good rider, and as I roamed the countries of the United States, Mexico, and Canada, riding for the big cow and horse outfits of them countries I rode many a different horse in as many a different place and fix. There was times when the horse under me meant my life, specially

15

once in Old Mexico, that once I sure can't forget, and then again, crossing the deserts I did cross, most always in strange territory and no arrows pointing as to the where-abouts of moisture, I had to depend altogether on the good horse under me whether the next water was twelve or sometimes forty-eight hours away.

With all the rambling I done which was for no reason at all only to fill the craving of a cowpuncher what always wanted to drift over that blue ridge ahead, my life was pretty well with my horse and I found as I covered the country, met different folks, and seen many towns, that the pin-eared pony under me (whichever one it was) was a powerful friend, powerful in confidence and strength. There was no suspicious question asked by him, nor "when do we eat." His rambling qualities was all mine to use as I seen fit, and I never abused it which is why I can say that I never was set afoot. Sometimes I had horses that was sort of fidgety and was told they'd leave me first chance they got whether they was hobbled or not but somehow I never was left, not even when the feed was scattered and no water for 'em to drink, and I've had a few ponies on such long cross-country trails that stayed close to camp with nothing on 'em that'd hinder 'em from hitting out if they wanted to.

A horse got to mean a heap more to me than just an animal to carry me around, he got to be my friend, I went fifty-fifty with him, and even though some showed me fight and I treated 'em a little rough there'd come a time when we'd have an understanding and we'd agree that we was both pretty good fellers after all.

And now that things are explained some, it all may be understood why running mustangs, catching 'em, and sell-ing 'em to any hombre that wanted 'em kind of got under my skin and where I live. I didn't see why I should help catch and make slaves out of them wild ones that was so free. Any and all of 'em was my friends—they was horse-flesh.

The boys wasn't at all pleased when I told 'em I'd decided to leave and wanted to know why, but I kept my sentiments to myself and remarked that I'd like to go riding for a cow outfit for a change. That seemed to satisfy 'em some and when they see I was bound to go they didn't argue. We started to divvy up the amount of ponies caught so as I'd get my share, and figgered fourteen head was coming to me. There was two days' catch already in the round corral of the trap and from that little bunch we picked out them I was to get.

There was a black stud in that bunch that I couldn't help but notice—I'd kept track of him ever since he was spotted the day before. He was young and all horse, and acted like he had his full share of brains. I wondered some how he come to get caught, and then again I had to size up the trap noticing how easy a horse, even a human, could be fooled, so well we'd built it.

The big main corral took in over an acre of ground; the fine, strong woven wire fastened on the junipers and piñons wasn't at all to be seen, specially by horses going at full speed, and the strength and height of that fence would of held a herd of stampeding buffalo.

Knowing that trap as I did, it was no wonder after all that black horse *was* caught. Nothing against his thinking ability, I thought, and as I watches him moving around wild-eyed seeming like to take a last long look at the steep hills he knowed so well I finds myself saying, "Little horse, I'm daggone sorry I helped catch you."

Right then I wanted that black horse, and I was sure going to get him if I could. I maneuvers around a lot and finally decides to offer the boys any three of the wild ones that'd been turned over to me as my share in trade for the black. It rook a lot of persuading, 'cause that black stud ranked way above the average, but the boys seeing that I wanted him so bad and me offering one more horse for him which made four, thought best to let me have him.

17

Will James

It was early the next morning when the black and the other ten horses I still had left was started away from the trap. Three of the boys was helping me keep 'em together, and as the wild ones all had to have one front foot tied up, it hindered 'em considerable to go faster than a walk, but that's what we wanted. We traveled slow and steady. The ponies tried to get away often, but always there was a rider keeping up with 'em on easy lope, and they finally seen where they had to give in and travel along the way *we* wanted 'em.

Fifteen miles or so away from the trap and going over a low summit, we get sight of a small high-fenced pasture, and to one side was the corrals. There was a cabin against the aspens and as I takes in the layout I recognizes it to be one of the Three T's Cattle Company's cow camps.

I decided we'd gone far enough with them horses for one day, so we corralled 'em there, and the boys went back after me telling 'em the ponies was herd-broke enough so I could handle 'em the next day by my lonesome, but they was some dubious about one man being able to do all that, even *if* the wild ones was tired, one foot tied up, and not aching to run.

The cabin was deserted, and I was glad of it, for I wasn't wanting company right then, I wanted to think. I went to sleep thinking and dreamt I was catching wild horses by the hundreds, and selling 'em to big slough-footed "haw-nyawks" what started beating 'em over the heads with clubs. I caught one big white stud and he just followed me in the trap. It all struck me as too easy to catch 'em, and the little money I was getting for 'em turned out to be a scab on my feelings compared to the price freedom was worth to them ponies.

I woke up early next morning and the memory of that dream was still with me, and when I pulled on my boots, built a fire and put on the coffee, I had visions of that black horse in the corral looking through a collar and pulling a plow in Alabama or some other such country.

18

I went outside, and while waiting for the coffee to come to a boil I struts out to the corral to take a look at the ponies. They're all bunched up, heads down, and ganted up, but soon as they see me they start milling, all heads up and a-snorting. I looks through the corral bars at 'em and watches 'em.

The black stud is closest to me and kinda protecting the mares and younger stock, there's a look in his eye that kinda reminds me of a man waiting for a sentence from the judge, only the spirit is still there and mighty challenging the same as to say, "What did I do?"

A little two-year-old filly slides up alongside of him and stares at me. I can see fear in her eyes and a kinda innocent wondering as to what this was all about, this being run into a trap, roped, a foot tied up, and then drove into another place with *bars* around.

All is quiet for a spell in the corral, a meadow lark is tuning up on a fence post close by, and with the light morning breeze coming through the junipers and piñons there's a feeling for everything that lives to just sun itself, listen, and breathe in.

Then it came to me how one time I'd got so homesick for just what I was experiencing right then, the country, and everything that was in it—I'd been East to a big town and got stranded there—that I'd given my right arm just so I got back.

When I come to and looked back in the corral, the black horse was looking way over the bars to the top of a big ridge. Out there was a small bunch of mustangs enjoying their freedom for all they was worth. So far there was no chance of a collar for them, and whether it was imagination or plain facts that I could see in that black stud's face, I sure made it out that he understood all that he was seeing was *past*, the shady junipers, the mountain streams, green grass and white sage was all to be left behind, even his little bunch of mares was going to be separated from him and took to goodness knows where.

Will James

Yes, sir! Thinking it all over that way sure made it hard to take. I didn't want to get sentimental, but daggone it I couldn't help but realize that I was the judge sentencing 'em to confinement and hard labor just for the few lousy dollars they'd bring.

Sure enough, *I* was the judge and could do as I blamed please. It struck me queer that it didn't come to me sooner.

I wasn't hesitating none as I picked up my rope and opened the gate into the corral, I worked fast as I caught each wild one, throwed him and took off the rope that was fastened from the tail to the front foot.

They was all foot-loose excepting the black. I hadn't

passed judgment on him as yet, but I knowed he wasn't going to be shipped to no cotton field, and the worst that could come his way would be to break him for my own saddle horse.

I opened the corral gate and lets the others out, watches 'em a spell, then turns to watch the black. "Little horse," I says to him, "your good looks and build are against you—"

But it was sure hard to let the others go and keep him in that way, it didn't seem square and the little horse was sure worrying about his bunch leaving him all by his lonesome, in a big corral with a human, and then I thinks of all the saddle horses I already had, of all the others I could get

that's been raised under fence and never knowed wild freedom.

Then my rope sings out once more, in no time his front foot is loose, the gate is open, and nothing in front of him but the high ridges of the country he knowed so well.

For a second I feel like kicking myself for letting such a horse go. He left me and the corral seemed like without touching the earth, floating out a ways, then turned and stood on his tiptoes, shook his head at me, let out a long whistle the same as to say "this is sure a surprise" and away he went, right on the trail his mares had took.

My heart went up my throat for a minute, I'd never seen a prettier picture to look at than that horse when he ambled away. The sight of him didn't seem to fit in with a saddle on his back and a heap less with a collar around his neck and following furrows instead of the mountain trails he was to run on once more.

I felt some relieved and thankful as I started back for the cabin. The coffee had boiled over while I was at the corral, and put the fire out, but I finds myself whistling and plumb contented with everything in general as I gathers kindling and starts the fire once again.

It was a few days later when I rides in on one of the Three T's roundup wagons, gets a job, a good string of company ponies, and goes to work. The wagon was on a big circle and making a new camp every day towards the mustang territory.

I was trying to get used to riding for a cow outfit once more, and it was hard. I'd find myself hankering to run mustangs but then I'd see them wild ponies crowded into stock cars and my hankering would die down sudden.

One day a couple of the boys rode up to the parada (main herd) from circle with a very few head of stock and it set me to wondering how come their horses could be so tired in that half-a-day's ride, but I didn't have to wonder long, for soon as they got near me one of 'em says, "We seen him!"

"Seen who?" I asks.

"Why, that black stud Midnight. Ain't you ever heard of him?"

"I don't know," I says, but it wasn't just a few minutes till I did know.

From all I was told right then it seemed like that Midnight horse was sure a wonder. It was rumored he was at least a half standard, but nobody was worried about that, the main thing was that he could sure run and what's more, keep it up.

"We spotted him early this morning," says one of the boys, "and soon as we did we naturally forgot all about cows. We took turns relaying on him. We had fast horses too, but we'd just as well tried to relay after a runaway locomotive."

I learned he had been caught once and broke to ride, but his mammy was a mustang, he'd been born and raised on the high pinnacles of the wild horse country, and one day when his owner thought it was safe to turn him out in a small pasture for a chance at green grass the horse just up and disappeared. The fences he had to cross to the open country never seemed to hinder him, and even though he was some three hundred miles from his home range, it was but a week or so later when some rider spotted him there again.

A two hundred dollar reward was offered for anyone that caught him. Many a good horse was tired out by different riders trying to get near him, traps was built, but Midnight had been caught once, and the supposed-to-be-wise fox was dumb compared to that horse.

I was getting right curious about then, and finally I asks for a full description of that flying hunk of horseflesh.

I'm holding my breath some as I'm told that his weight is around eleven hundred, pure black, and perfect built, and a small brand on his neck right under his mane, a "C."

Yep! that was him, none other than that black horse I turned loose.

Will James

I started wondering how *we* caught him so easy, but a vision of that trap came to me again. It wasn't at all like the traps other mustangers of that country ever built, and that's what got Midnight. We had him thinking he was getting away from us easy, when at the same time he was running right inside the strong, invisible, net fence.

A picture of him came to my mind as he looked when I turned him loose that day now a couple of weeks past, and then I thought of the two hundred that was offered to anybody who'd run him in. That was a lot of money for a mustang, but somehow it didn't seem to be much after all, not comparing with Midnight.

It was late in the fall when I seen the black stud again. Him and his little bunch was sunning themselves on the side of a high ridge. A sarvisberry bush was between me and them, and tying my horse to a juniper, I sneaks up towards 'em, making sure to keep out of sight. I figgered I'd be about two hundred yards from the bunch once I got near the berry bush, but when I got there and straightened up to take a peek through the branches, the wild bunch had plumb evaporated off the earth. I could see for a mile around me but all I could tell of the whereabouts of Midnight and his mares was a light dust away around the point of the ridge.

"Pretty wise horse," I thinks, but somehow I felt relieved a lot to know he was going to make himself mighty hard to catch.

The winter that came was a tough one, the snow was deep and grass was hard to get. I was still riding for the Three T's outfit and was kept mighty busy bringing whatever stock I'd find what needed feed, and as I was riding the country for such and making trails out for snowbound cattle I had a good chance to watch how the wild horses was making it.

They wasn't making it very good, and as the already long winter seemed to never want to break I noticed that the bunches was getting smaller, many of the old mares layed down never to get up, and the coyotes was getting fat.

24

Midnight

Midnight and his bunch was nowheres to be seen, and I got kind of worried that some hombre wanting that two hundred dollars right bad had started out after him with grain-fed horses, and the black horse being kinda weaker on account of the grass being hard to get at might've let a rope sneak up on him and draw up around his neck.

I knowed of quite a few riders that calculated to get him that winter, and I knowed that if he wasn't already caught, he'd sure been fogged a good many times.

I often wished that I'd hung on to him while I had him, and give him as much freedom as I could, just so nobody pestered him. I'd forgot that the horse already belonged to somebody else and I'd have to give him up anyway, but that pony had got under my skin pretty deep. I just wanted to do a good turn to horseflesh in general by leaving him and all the other wild ones as they was.

Winter finally broke up and spring with warm weather had come, when as I'm riding along one day tailing up weak stock, I finds that all my worries about the black stud getting caught was for nothing.

I was in the bottom of a boggy wash helping a bellering critter up on her feet. As luck would have it my horse was hid, and as for me, only my head was sticking up above the bank, when I happened to notice the little wild bunch filing in towards me from over a low ridge. I recognized Midnight's mares by their color and markings, but I couldn't make out that shaggy, faded, long-haired horse trailing in along behind quite a ways. He was kind of a dirty brown.

I stood there in the mud up above my ankles and plumb forgot the wild-eyed cow that was so much in need of a boost to dry ground, all my interest was for spotting Midnight, and my heart went up my throat as I noticed the faded brown horse. That couldn't be Midnight, I thought, Midnight must of got caught some way and this shadow of a horse just naturally appropriated the bunch.

But as I keeps on watching 'em trail in and getting closer there's points about that shaggy pony in the rear that strikes me familiar. He looks barely able to pack his own weight, and his weight wasn't much right then for I could see his ribs mighty plain even through the long winter hair. All the other ponies had started to shed off some and was halfways slick, but not him.

The bunch was only a couple of ropes' length away from me as they trailed in the boggy wash to get a drink of the snow water, and I had to hug the bank to keep out of sight and stick my head in a sagebrush so as I could see without them seeing me.

Then I recognized Midnight. That poor son of a gun was sure well disguised with whatever ailed him, and when I got a good look at that head of his I thought sure a rattler had bit him. His jaws and throat was all swelled up plumb to his ears, but as I studies him I seen it wasn't a snake's doings. It was distemper at its worst, and the end was as sure as if he'd been dead unless I could catch him and take care of him.

I'm out on my best horse the next morning, and making sure the corral gate was wide open and the wings to it in good shape I headed for the quickest way of locating Midnight. I had no trouble there, and run onto him and his bunch when only a couple of hours away from camp.

I thought he was weak enough so I could ride right in on him and rope him on the spot, but I was fooled mighty bad. He left me like I was standing still, and tail up he headed for the roughest country he could find, me right after him.

My horse was grain-fed, steady, strong, and in fine shape to run, but as the running kept up over washouts, mountains, and steep ridges for the big part of that day, I seen where there was less hope of ever getting within roping distance of the black.

Daggone that horse anyway. I was finding myself cussing and admiring him at the same time. I was afraid he'd run himself to death rather than let any rider get near him, and I thought some of letting him go, only I knowed the distemper would kill him sure, and I wanted to save him.

I made a big circle and covered a lot of territory, my horse was getting mighty tired, and as I pushed on the trail of Midnight and got to within a few miles of my camp, I branched off and let him go. I was going to get me a fresh horse.

I was on his trail again by sundown, and an hour or so later a big moon came up to help me keep track of the dust Midnight was making. That big moon was near halfways up the sky when I begins to see signs of the black horse weakening. I feels mighty sorry for the poor devil right then, and as I uncoils my rope and gets ready to dab it on him I says to him, "Midnight, old horse, I'm only trying to help you."

Then my rope sails out and snares him. He didn't fight as I drawed up my slack and stopped him, instead his head hung down near the ground and if I ever seen a picture marking the end of the trail, there was one.

It was daybreak as we finally reached the corral and sheds of my camp. In a short while I'd lanced and doctored up his throat, good as any vet could of done, made him swallow a good stiff dose of medicine I had on hand for that purpose in case any of my ponies ever got layed up that way, and seeing he had plenty to eat and drink in case he'd want it I started towards the cabin to cook me a bait. That done and consumed I caught me another fresh horse and rode out for that day's work.

I'd been doctoring up on Midnight for a week without sign he ever would recuperate. He was the same as the day I brought him in and I was getting scared that he never would come out of it. Every night and morning as I'd go to give him his medicine I'd stand there and watch him for a spell. He'd got used to that and being that my visits that way meant some relief to his suffering he got to looking for me, and would nicker kinda soft as he'd get sight of me.

If I could only get him to eat the grain I'd bring there'd

be a chance but he didn't seem to know what grain was, and from that I got the idea he hadn't been treated any too well that first time he was caught. I'd kept sprinkling some of that grain in the hay so as he'd get used to the taste and begin looking for it, but he wasn't eating much hay and it took quite a long time before I begin noticing that the grain I'd put in the box had been touched. From then on, he started eating it and gradually got so he'd clean up all I'd give him.

There was the beginning of a big change in the little horse after that. The powders I'd mix in the grain started to working on him, the swelling on his neck went down, his eyes showed brighter, and he begin to shed the long faded winter hair. After that it was easy, a couple of weeks more care and he was strong as ever again, all he needed was the green grass that was all over hills by now. It was time for me to turn him loose—and that's what I did.

It was near sundown when I led him out from under the shed, through the corral where I'd let him out of once before near a year past, and on out to where he'd be free to go. I took the hackamore off his head—nothing was holding him—but this time he just stood there, his head was high and his eyes was taking in the big country around him.

He spoke plainer than a human when, after taking long appreciating breaths of the cool spring air, he sniffed at my shoulder and looked up the hills again. He wasn't wondering or caring if I understood him so long as he understood me, and that he did—he knowed I was with him for all the freedom these valleys and mountains could give him.

It was a couple of months later when one of the cowboys rode up to my camp on his way to the home ranch, stopped with me a night, and before he left the next morning dropped me some information that caused me to do a heap of thinking.

It appeared like some outfit had moved in on this range and was going to clean it out of all the wild horses that was

28

on it. They had permits and contracts to do that and seemed like the capital to go through with it. Most of 'em was foreign hombres that craved for other excitements than just jazz, and getting tired of spending their old man's money all in one place had framed it up to come West and do all that *for a change*.

They was bringing along some fast thoroughbreds, and I couldn't help but wonder how long them poor spindle-legged ponies would last in these rocks and shale. They'd be as helpless as the hombres riding 'em. If it'd been only them highbloods I'd just laughed and felt mighty safe for the wild ones, but no such luck, they was paying top wages and hiring the best mustang runners in the country.

As I heard it from that cowboy it was sure some expensive layout, there was big wagonloads of fancy grub and fancier drinks, air mattresses and pillows, tents and folding bathtubs and tables, perfume and chewing gum, etc., etc.—Yep! they was going to *rough it*.

"But I'm thinking," says the cowboy as he left, "that with the wild horse hunters they hired, that black stud Midnight is going to find hisself in a trap once more, and somehow I'd kinda hate to see them catch that horse."

For a few weeks that outfit was busy building traps. I seen they was going at it big as I rode through one of 'em one day, and as I talked to one of the pilgrims who I'd found busy picking woodticks out of his brand-new Angora chaps, I also seen they had big visions of cleaning this country of the mustangs along with making a potful of money.

"And it's the greatest sport I know of," says that hombre as he reaches for another woodtick next to his ear.

"Yeh," I says to myself as I rides away, "I'm not wishing him harm, but I hope he breaks his neck at it."

There was in the neighborhood of a thousand head of mustangs in that country, and it wasn't long when the hills and white sage flats was being tore by running hoofs, a steady haze of fine dust was floating in the air and could be seen for miles around, and at night I could see signal fires. Some greenhorn had got lost or set afoot.

The hired mustang runners was having a hard time of it; one told me one day they'd of caught twice as many if them pilgrims wasn't around. "Two of the boys was bringing in a nice bunch yesterday," he was saying. "They had 'em to within a few yards of the gate and as good as caught, when up from behind a rock jumps a pilgrim and hollers, 'That's the good boys, step on 'em!' Well, the ponies turned quicker than a flash and *they* done all the stepping, a good thirty head got away."

I was glad to hear that in a way, but I was careful not to show it. I was thinking that after all Midnight and his little bunch had a chance at their freedom, and I finds myself whistling a pretty lively tune as I rode on.

I hadn't seen Midnight only once since I turned him loose that last time, and I had a hunch that he'd changed his range on account of these mustangers keeping him on the dodge, but then again this wasn't the only outfit that was out for the wild ones. The whole country for a hundred miles around was full of riders out for the fuzztails (mustangs), and I couldn't figger out where that horse and his little bunch could go where they'd be safe.

But nobody had seen the black stud, and everybody was wanting him. I was asked often if I'd seen any sign of him, and as I'd go on a-riding the country keeping tab on the company's cattle that was on the same range as the wild ones, I was watching steady for him, but he couldn't be seen anywheres.

Come a time when it was easy to notice that the mustangs was fast disappearing. I could ride for a week at a stretch without seeing more than a few head where some months before I could of counted hundreds. I'd run acrost little colts, too young to keep up and left behind. Their mammies had stayed with 'em long as they could but as the riders would gain on 'em fast, fear would get the best of 'em, and the poor little devils would be left behind to shift for themselves before they was able to, and keep a-nickering and a-circling for the mammy that never came back. She'd be in the trap.

Carloads of wild ones was being shipped every month to all points of the U. S. wherever there was a market for 'em. They was sold to farmers and drug to the farm back of a wagon, the trip in the stock cars, not mentioning their experiences in the trap, took most of the heart out of 'em, and there was no fight much as the collar was slipped around their necks and hooked up alongside the gentle farm horse—a big change from the tall peaks, mountain streams near hid with quaking asp, bunch grass, and white sage.

It was late fall and the air was getting mighty crimpy when the mustang-running outfits started pulling up their tent pins and moving out, the country looked mighty silent and deserted and all the black dots that could be seen at a distance wasn't mustangs no more, it was mighty safe to say that them black dots was cattle. . . .

I rides up to the pilgrim camp one day just as one of 'em is putting away his cold cream and snake-bite outfit, and inquires how they all enjoyed the country and mustang trapping.

"Oh, the country is great, and mustang trapping is a ripping sport," I'm told, "but we lost a few thousand dollars on the deal which don't make it so good. Besides our blooded horses are ruined.

"And by the way," goes on that same hombre, "have you seen that black stallion they call Midnight anywheres? I see by the San Jacinto *News* that the reward on the horse is withdrawn, also the ownership, so he is free to anyone who catches him, I understand."

"Yes," I says, tickled to death at the news, "but there's a catch to it and that's *catching him.*"

"Free to anyone who catches him," stayed in my mind for a good many days, but where could that son of a gun be?

Will James

I tried to think of all the hiding spots there was, I knowed 'em all well, I thought, but I also knowed that all them hiding spots had been rode into and the mustangs there had been caught. I was getting mighty worried that Midnight and his little bunch might by now be somewheres where the fences are thick and the fields are small, a couple of thousand miles away.

It's early one morning when I notices one of my saddle horses had got through the pasture fence and left. Soon I was on his trail to bring him back, and that trail led through the aspens back of my cabin and on up to a big granite ledge where it was lost on the rocky ground. Figgering on making a short cut to where I can spot that pony, I leaves my horse tied to a buckbrush and climbs over the granite ledge. When I gets up there, there's another ledge, and then another one, and by the time I gets to the top of all of 'em I'm pretty high.

I was some surprised to find a spring up there, fine clear water that run only a short ways and sunk in the ground again, but what surprised me most was the horse tracks around it. How could a horse ever get up here, I thought, but they was here sure enough. I noticed the feed was awful short and scarce and I wondered if it was because them horses couldn't get down as easy as they got up.

Investigating around and looking over big granite boulders I can make out horses' backs a-shining in the sun. They're feeding in their small territory, and I can tell they're feeling pretty safe, but as I moves around, a head comes up, ears pointed my way, and wild eyes a staring at me.

In that second I recognized the black stud Midnight.

There's a loud snort and whistle, and like a bunch of quail Midnight and his bunch left that spot for higher ground and where they could see all around 'em, but a man afoot was something new and not so much to run away from, and finally they stood off at a good distance and watched me.

The surprise of finding Midnight, and so close to my

camp, left me able to do nothing but set where I was and do my share of watching. In a little while I started talking to him and I could see he sure remembered and recognized me. His wild look disappeared and he made a half circle as if to come my way. I wished he'd come closer, but I hadn't broke him to that. I hadn't broke him to anything, I'd only tried to give him to understand that he was safe of that freedom as long as he lived.

I knowed he understood ever since that second time I turned him loose. The proof of that was him picking his hiding place as close to my camp as he could get while the mustang runners was in the country. I know he'd been there all the last few months, and I know there was many a time when he looked down on my cabin, which was only a half a mile or so away, while I was wondering where he could be.

I seen him looking down at me that way the next morning. He was hard to see amongst the scrub mahogany, but it's a wonder, I thought, why it never come to me to look up there.

Somehow or other, Midnight and his bunch got down off their hiding place. The mustang runners had all left the country, and as I rode up on the small bunch of remaining wild ones one day and watched 'em lope away toward the flat, I knowed they was safe.

I knowed they'd come back if they ever got crowded, and to that hiding place which nobody else knowed of but us 'uns.

THE WINNING OF DARK BOY

JOSEPHINE NOYES FELTS

I don't believe it. I just don't believe it!" whispered Ginger Grey to herself as she watched Dark Boy, the beautiful black steeplechaser, going round and round on the longe, the training rope to which he was tethered in the O'Malleys' yard. She was stroking him with her eyes, loving every curve, every flowing muscle of his slender, shining body.

But the voice of Tim O'Malley, Dark Boy's owner, still echoed in her ears. "You're a brave little horsewoman, Ginger, but Dark Boy would kill you. I'm getting rid of him next week. He's thrown three experienced men and run away twice since I've had him. You are not to get on him!"

Ginger wiped a rebellious tear from her cheek, looking quickly around to make sure that neither ten-year-old Tommy nor the two younger children had seen her. She was alone at the O'Malley farm, several miles away from home, looking after the O'Malley children for the day while their father and mother were in town. Why couldn't she have had the exercising and training of this glorious horse! Her heart ached doubly, for she longed to ride him next week in the horse show at Pembroke.

Ginger glanced now at the two little girls playing in the yard. They needed their noses wiped. She took care of this, patted them gently, and went back to where Dark Boy was loafing at the end of the longe. He didn't seem to mind the light saddle she had put on him. The reins of the bridle trailed the ground. She must go soon and take it off. He'd had a good workout today, she thought with satisfaction. Exercise was what he needed. And now with nobody riding him . . .

She shivered suddenly and noticed how much colder it had turned. A great bank of black clouds had mounted up over the woods behind the meadow. She studied the clouds anxiously. Bad storms sometimes rose quickly out of that corner of the sky. The air seemed abnormally still, and there was a weird copper light spreading from the west.

If it was going to storm she'd better get the children in the house, put Dark Boy in the barn, and find Tommy. Here came Tommy now, dirty, tousled, one leg of his jeans torn and flapping as he walked.

"Barbed wire," he explained cheerfully, pointing to his pants. "Zigafoos has fenced his fields with it!"

A sharp gust of wind rounded the house. Tommy flapped in it like a scarecrow. A shutter on the house banged sharply; the barn door creaked shrilly as it slammed. Dark Boy reared and thudded to the ground.

"Look!" yelled Tommy suddenly. "What a close funny cloud!"

A thin spiral of smoke was rising from behind the O'Malleys' barn. Ginger's heart froze within her. Fire! She raced around the barn. Then she saw with horror that the lower part of that side was burning. The wind must have blown a spark from a smoldering trash pile. Already the blaze was too much for anything she and Tommy could do. She'd have to get help at once!

As she tore back toward the house, pictures flashed through her mind. The big red fire truck was in the village six miles down the road. There were no phones. Any cars in the scattered neighborhood would be down in the valley with the men who used them to get to work at the porcelain factory. She'd have to get to the village and give the fire alarm herself immediately. Perhaps on Dark Boy . . .

She dashed over to him and caught his bridle. He tossed his head and sidled away from her, prancing with excitement. As she talked quietly to him, with swift fingers she loosened the longe, letting it fall to the ground. She felt sure that she could guide him if only she could get on him and stay on him when he bolted. She thrust her hand deep in her pocket and brought out two of the sugar lumps she had been saving for him.

"Sugar for a good boy," she panted and reached up to his muzzle. Dark Boy lipped the sugar swiftly, his ears forward.

With a flying leap Ginger was up, had swung her right leg over him and slipped her right foot in the stirrup. She sat lightly forward as jockeys do. Would he resent her? Throw her off? Or could she stick?

Indignant, Dark Boy danced a wide circle of astonishment. The wind was whistling furiously now around the house, bending the trees. Ginger held the reins firmly and drew Dark Boy to a prancing halt. Then, suddenly, he reared. She clung with her lithe brown knees and held him tight. Precious minutes were flying. She thought of the bright tongues of flame licking up the side of the barn.

"Tommy! Take care of the children!" she shouted over her shoulder as Dark Boy angrily seized the bit between his teeth and whirled away. "I'll get help!"

Ginger's light figure in a red blob of sweater flashed down the road through the twisting trees. Fast as Dark Boy's bright hooves beat a swift rhythm on the hard clay road, Ginger's thoughts raced ahead. She glanced at her watch. By the road it was six miles to the town. At Dark Boy's throbbing gallop they might make it in fifteen minutes. By the time the fire department got back it might well be much too late.

There was a crash like thunder off in the woods to her

left as the first dead tree blew down. Dark Boy shied violently, almost throwing her headlong, but she bent lower over his neck and clung. Suddenly her heart stiffened with dread. What had she done! She'd been wrong to leave the children. Suppose Tommy took them into the house, and the house caught fire from the barn! She hadn't thought of the wind and the house. She'd only thought of saving the barn!

Desperately she pulled at Dark Boy's mouth. But he was going at a full runaway gallop, the bit between his teeth. Stop now? Go back? No!

There was one way that she might save precious seconds: take him across the fields, the short cut, the way the children went to school. That way it was only two miles! There were fences between the fields, but Dark Boy was a steeplechaser and trained to jump. She'd have to take a chance on jumping him now. They thundered toward the cutoff.

Peering ahead for fallen trees as the branches groaned and creaked above her, she guided him into the little lane that ran straight into a field where the main road turned sharply. Now he was responding to her touch, his great muscles flowing under his glossy coat like smoothly running water. She held him straight toward the stile at the far end of the field. Here was the place to take their first jump. Would he shy before it and make them lose the moments they were saving? Or would he take it smoothly?

She leaned anxiously forward and patted Dark Boy's silky neck. "Straight into it, beautiful! Come on, Boy!"

Dark Boy laid back an ear as he listened. A few yards ahead of the stile she tightened the reins, lifted his head, and rose lightly in the stirrups. Dark Boy stretched out his neck, left the ground almost like a bird, she thought. His bright hooves cleared the stile.

"Wonderful, beautiful Boy!" Ginger cried as they thudded on.

40

Now to the second fence! Over it they went, smooth as silk. Her heart lifted.

Down below them in the valley the little town of Honeybrook flashed in and out of sight behind the tortured trees. She thought briefly of the steep bank from the lower field onto the road below. What would Dark Boy do there? Would he go to pieces and roll as horses did sometimes to get down steep banks? Or could she trust him, count on his good sense, hold him firmly while he put his feet together and slid with her safely to within reach of the fire alarm?

They were headed now across a rounded field. Dark Boy lengthened his glistening neck, stretched his legs in a high gallop. Just then, irrelevantly, Tommy flashed into Ginger's mind, his torn jeans flapping in the wind. "Barbed wire! Oh, Dark Boy!"

Here was a danger she had not considered, a danger that stretched straight across their path, one she could not avoid! The lower end of Zigafoos' field, the one they were crossing now at such headlong speed, was fenced with it. Dark Boy couldn't possibly see it! This time she would be helpless to lift him to the jump. He'd tear into it, and at this pace he would be killed. She would never give her warning. Her heart beating wildly, she pulled the reins up to her chest.

"This way, Boy!" turning his head.

He curved smoothly. There weren't two of them now; horse and rider were one. They made the wide circle of the field. First at a gallop, then dropping to a canter and a walk. She stopped him just in time. He was quivering, shaking his head, only a few feet from the nearly invisible, vicious wire. As she slid to her feet the wind threw her against him.

"Here, Boy, come on," she urged breathlessly. Dark Boy, still trembling, followed her. She skinned out of her sweater and whipped its brilliant red over the barbed wire, flagging it for him. "There it is, Boy, now we can see it!"

Dark Boy was breathing heavily. Without protest this

41

time, he let her mount. She dug her heels into his flanks and put him back into a gallop for the jump. Amid a thunder of hooves she took him straight for the crimson marker. Dark Boy lifted his feet almost daintily, stretched out his head, and they were clear!

He galloped now across the sloping field. "Good Boy, good Boy!" she choked, patting his foaming withers as he stretched out on the last lap of their race against fire and time.

The wind was still sharp in her face, but the terrifying black clouds had veered to the south, traveling swiftly down the Delaware valley. She could see distinctly the

spire of the old church rising above the near grove of trees. How far beneath them it still seemed! That last fifty feet of the trail they would have to slide.

"Come on!" she urged, holding the reins firmly, digging her heels into his flanks to get one last burst of speed from his powerful frame. They flew along the ledge. Ahead in the clearing she could see the long bank that dropped to the road leading into the town. Just under top runaway speed but breathing hard, Dark Boy showed that the race was telling on him. With gradual pressure she began to pull him in.

"Slow, Boy, slow," she soothed. "You're doing fine!

Don't overshoot the mark. Here we are, old fellow. Slide!''

His ears forward, his head dipped, looking down, quivering in every inch of his spent flanks, Dark Boy responded to the pressure of her knees and hands. Putting his four feet together, he half slid, half staggered down the bank and came to a quivering stop on the empty village street not ten feet from the great iron ring that gave the fire alarm. He was dripping and covered with foam.

As Ginger's hand rose and fell with the big iron clapper, the clang of the fire alarm echoed, and people ran to their doors. The alarm boomed through the little covered bridge up to Smith's machine shop. The men working there heard it, and dropping their tools, came running, not bothering to take off their aprons. It rang out across Mrs. Harnish's garden. Mr. Harnish and the oldest Harnish boy heard it and vaulted lightly over the fence, then ran, pulling on their coats.

While the big red engine roared out of the Holms' garage and backed up toward the canal bridge to get under way, Ginger called out the location of the fire. She fastened Dark Boy securely to a fence and climbed into the fire truck. They roared away up the hill.

Ginger looked at her watch again. In just eight minutes she and Dark Boy had made their race through the storm. It seemed eight hours! A few more minutes would tell whether or not they had won.

"Please, God," Ginger whispered, "take care of Tommy and the girls!"

They slowed briefly at Erwin's corner to pick up two more volunteers, then sent the big red truck throbbing up Turtle Hill. Tears trickled down between Ginger's fingers. Ned Holm threw an arm gently around her shoulders.

"Good girl!" he said smiling at her reassuringly. "We go the hill up! We get there in time!"

Ginger shook the tears from her eyes and thanked him

with a smile. But at the wheel Rudi set his lips in a grim line as he gave the truck all the power it had and sent it rocking over the rough road. The siren screamed fatefully across the valley. A barn can burn in little time and catch a house, too, if the wind is right, and this wind was right!

"How'd you come?" he growled.

"Across the fields—on Dark Boy."

"Dark Boy!" Rudi's eyes narrowed and he held them fixed on the road as he steered.

Ned Holm gasped. "You mean that steeplechaser nobody can stay on?"

"I stayed on!"

They rounded the turn at the top of the hill. Now they could see the great black cloud of smoke whirling angrily over the O'Malleys' trees. As they came to a throbbing stop in the O'Malleys' yard and the men set up the pump at the well, a corner of the house burst into flames. Five minutes more and . . . !

Tommy ran panic-stricken toward them. The barn was blazing fiercely now and in a little while all that would be left of it would be the beautiful Pennsylvania Dutch stonework. A stream of water played over the house. Sparks were falling thick and fast but the stream was soaking the shingles.

Ginger caught Tommy in her arms. "Where are the kids?" she shouted.

"In—in the house. I carried them up and then put the fence at the stairs. They don't like it much!"

Ned Holm ran with Ginger up the steep, narrow stairs and helped her carry out the squirming, indignant children.

That night when the fire was out and the big O'Malleys were home, the little O'Malleys safely in bed, Ginger at home told her mother all about the day. She was a little relieved that nobody scolded her about riding Dark Boy. Her mother just cried a little and hugged her.

Next morning they saw Tim O'Malley riding Dark Boy up the Greys' lane. Ginger raced out to meet him. Tim swung down and led the black horse up to Ginger.

"Here's your horse," he said simply. "You've won him!"

Ginger stared at him speechless.

Tim went on. "I want you to ride Dark Boy next week in the Pembroke show. And I expect you to win!"

"We'll try, sir," said Ginger.

MORENA

PAUL ZACHARY COHEN

(an excerpt)

T he horse slowly ambling amid the high, rough reaches of the Finger Hills was alone, because she had slipped through the busyness and the galloping and the shouting that had driven away the other four horses and the whole steer herd, a month before.

She was no longer as fast as the roundup, but she had lived for twenty-four years. She had learned that the startlingly loud waves of a man's hat were only the waves of a hat. She had learned to know when she'd be chased if she cut back, and when the ridden horses were too busy. She had learned which trees, in which draws, in which angles of the sunlight, would conceal her. Once hidden, she had the advantage of not being in a hurry.

She had not only avoided the roundup, but had escaped the deer hunters who had glimpsed her, and also the single, familiar man on horseback who had hounded her close for two days. She had escaped the hunters quickly, not knowing they'd turned back the moment a hoofprint and her fresh droppings had told them that what they'd seen was not a deer.

But the rider had several times forced her out of brush clumps, and into dodging gallops around them, and down through gully washes that made her strain and bruise her legs, until finally she'd found a place where he came no more.

"Stay here and freeze and starve!" he'd roared, though even to himself the rider had seemed to make scarcely any sound at all amid all the vast earth and sky. Then he'd ridden off. Out of his sight, Morena had rolled to dry off her sweat, and had lain down to rest, very wearied.

But now another familiar urging was upon her. She knew—perhaps from the lighter pressure of the calm air, or from the taste and swing of the winds that started and fell—that the first hard storm of the changing season was coming.

She'd begun walking. It was a slow, ambling, softly jolting gait: shoulders stiffly slipping frontward and back, hips rocking up and down in an old practiced rhythm. She was aware that, somehow, her rhythm was slower than it had once been, but she'd forget that and start to hurry. Then the ache of tiredness would start to grab her, and she'd slow down.

She kept moving along out in the open, following the beaten, easy grade of a cattle trail up a hill, then deserting the trail, knowing it led down into a draw whose brush was thick, and the cattle-tunnel through it too low. She followed the crest, then went down and crossed where the bottom brush was thinnest, humped and struggled up the other side, and ambled on.

She knew every turn and stretch of the paths to follow. She knew where openings in every pasture fence would be, and that the air on the lower plains would still be warm, and the haystacks there fresh-smelling. She knew she was starting back closer to men. But every touch of the air, every instinct inside her, warned it was death to remain. She must leave.

Then something went wrong. The gateway from the upper pasture was closed.

She moved this way and that in front of it. She pawed a little, nervously and restlessly. In twenty-four years she had had to make adjustments before, and she remembered that. Off she went, ambling up and down the hills, following

50

the fence line. But the other two gates on the lower side of the pasture were closed, too. And at the place where the wide, hard trail went through the open fence, there was always a big pit crossed by round bars that her hooves could not stand on. Twice she'd gotten her legs trapped down between those bars and the terror of that feeling she remembered well.

Back she came toward the main wire gate she was used to, trotting a little. She carried her head high above the top wire of the fence line, as if trying to hear or scent amid the air's warning some hint of explanation or escape, or as if by seeing over the problem, she might get by it.

The main gate was still closed.

She lowered her head to scratch against her forelegs. She looked up and sniffed again, and pawed, and moved about, but never far. She could no longer gather the kind of strength to try jumping that high. Nor was she panicked enough to crash through it blindly. She was restless, but otherwise she was comfortable enough for the moment.

She pawed out clumsily at the gate with her front hooves. Then she pecked at the grasses a little bit one way, a little bit another, but she stayed close to the gate and the blocked pathway that led through it. She could think of no other direction to go.

The afternoon dimmed and grew dark around her. Over beyond the high rise of the hills behind her, the approaching storm rolled and blossomed and swirled across the earth.

———————

At the Mallet Creek Campground, right where the high ridge timber dwindled out down the Finger Hills, two large, awkward yellow beasts started growling at each other. Then their headlights came on, and one behind the other the school buses began to slowly bounce along the rock roadway toward lower ground. The patches of embers left behind were drenched and mounded with the pebbly dirt and gave no glow. The back of each bus was piled high with tents and sleeping bags rolled up grudgingly, and thus somewhat sloppily. The night was the last of October—Halloween—and a spook, indeed, had caused this unwanted retreat: a spook in the shape of a little black box that had spoken with the voice of a man forty miles away in the radio station at Belle Ore. A man with a witch's voice that had cackled and sparked as he'd warned of heavy snow and high winds to come during the night.

The happy part was that it might make the teachers all late getting back from their yearly Friday-Saturday convention, but the combined Scout troops from Belle Ore and Alder Springs had groaned at the threat to the second night of their camp-out. They hadn't panicked, though. They had looked at the sky, tested the air, and decided there was time at least for the cookout—then the sing-out—and it was ten o'clock before the buses awoke and growled and left.

The rocky roadway soon became a little smoother and more gravelly. Then an eerie green needle on the dashboard of the second bus swung to the left; the bus immediately flickered its headlights and stopped. The first bus stopped, too, and the drivers got out and began a hurried conversation on the possibilities of an oil leak or perhaps just a crossed wire.

Lying cramped on a seat in that second bus, Alex Jaynes was especially hexed. Maybe it was a germ he'd brought with him, maybe it was the mulligan of hamburger, bouillon, mushroom soup, powdered potatoes, and powdered milk that he and Dale Logelin had used for their hurriedly cooked supper. But it was the greasy salt from the huge community bag of potato chips that he still tasted, and the sweet, half-cooled pop pulled from the creek.

The sick feeling had begun almost immediately after supper, and had kept at him so badly that Alex had passed up the first bus—the Alder bus—and the plans he'd had to spend Sunday with Dale. Dale could eat anything. But Alex'd gotten on the second bus, wanting only to get back to Belle Ore and to his grandparents for help. He'd pillowed his heavy jacket against the sharp window ledge, and wrapped in the cover of his light jacket, he'd sunk down across the whole seat. It had embarrassed him to claim such a privilege, and to let the misery show in his face, but that way he didn't have to try talking. The other kids had let him alone. They'd gone on with their talking and joking as if he wasn't there. And in the thick, awful air from the bus's heater his head had ached and his stomach had kept trying to throw the whole mess out on the floor, where it would stink accusingly at him the whole trip.

He'd held on while the bus was moving, and cool, clear air leaked in around the windows; but in the stagnant stillness of the pause, it became harder and harder. Around him the sounds of the talk and horseplay beat louder. The heat grew thick. Then the kids began to razz the delay by singing "Rolling home, rolling home, as we go rolling, rolling home—" louder and louder until finally Alex could take it no longer. He eased away from his seat and slipped out the door as unobtrusively as possible.

Outside, shielded by the darkness and the whirring of a steady wind and the rumbling of the motors, he took five, six steps, found a rock to support him, and let it come. The rush of acrid-tasting stuff filled his mouth and nose; and when it was done, his whole system kept kicking and sucking and tightening, and finally he threw up some more and then relaxed. Alex leaned back against the rock, feeling weak as a twig, and letting the cool, damp wind wash over him.

Then he saw Milt Toppen heading back into the Belle Ore bus, and Alex got up to go, too. When he moved, his stomach caught him, as if he were strapped to the rock; it squeezed in with a sharp breathless grip, and began retching dryly; Alex gasped and hung to the rock, bent double; still nothing came, but his muscles tensed and his head thickened painfully with the pressure. Thinly behind him he heard the swish and grumble of the brakes being released and the bus starting up. It was a moment before the fright of it reached him, a moment more before the retching quit. He turned, saw the bus moving, and ran after it.

"Hey!" he called out, with a shout.

A roar of changing gears and a thick breath of exhaust drowned him under.

He leaped ahead faster, caught up with the bus's rear end. He hit his hand twice against it. Inside he could hear another muffled chorus of "Rolling home, rolling home, as we go rolling, rolling home—." There was lots of loose gravel being tossed up anyway; his hand had made a noise, but not much of one on the heavy, rigid steel.

"*Hey!*" Alex screamed wildly this time, as the motor was gunned, and shot its exhaust at him, sourly. Very rapidly it was picking up speed, pulling just ten feet ahead, then twenty, closer to fifty, moving steadily, swiftly away, without stopping at all, but going farther and faster into the white sweep of headlights, the red taillights staring idiotically back at him. Alex finally stopped running; he simply couldn't believe it.

That was the first feeling, the disbelief. Then a tinge of panic, but Alex beat that quickly down with good humor.

"Well, nuts," he said, to an imaginary other self suddenly standing there inside him. "We're going to have to walk. I ought to yank out my stomach and make it walk, too. Why should I carry my stomach after it's done this?" He kept waiting every moment, for the bus to stop and wait for him.

It kept going.

The swift wind whistled close around him, not caring. The lights of the buses kept dashing and winking farther and farther away, silent and not caring. The ground felt hard beneath him. The stars were weak and few above the cool moistness of the wind. The friendly other self he tried to feel standing there inside him began to laugh: *"I'm* not really here, not really. You're all alone."

Alex felt the wind whip at him again, then grab at him, then swallow him whole as he tromped up out of the draw. It was a stronger wind than the one that had brought the snow, and now he was facing into it. It scraped his eyes so that they watered and blurred, and hurt his ears so that he tied his handkerchief around his head, but the wind went through it; then he dug his cold hands back deep in his hay-filled pockets.

Yet there was a little more spring in his legs. He didn't feel bad. Even the gray morning was cheerful after the hard and hostile night. He began telling himself, with amazement and pride, that he'd survived a night snowstorm out in the wilds all alone, with only his hiking clothes and a sheath knife. He felt that soon something—most likely a game warden's truck—would be beckoning him into its warmth. Meanwhile, that horse was standing there out in the open, not half a mile away.

He stayed upright, betting he had a better chance that way than trying to cover the distance creeping or crawling and looking like some animal no horse had ever seen before. Patiently and steadily he plodded ahead, through snow nearly as deep as his boot tops. He experimented with bobbing his head up and down, thinking he might accidently resemble another horse that way. With the wind pouring at him, there was no chance of the horse catching his scent.

The horse stood facing him, its head dropped low in the windbreak protection of his shoulders. Alex hoped that it was not a stallion, and the thin look of the shoulders seemed to promise it was not. Gradually now as he moved, he reached under his light jacket and unbuckled his belt and freed his sheath knife. He put the knife into his hip pocket, handle down to help keep it from falling out. He left the belt loose in its loops, ready to be slipped out and around the horse's neck.

He was about halfway to the horse.

Suddenly it looked up, ears perked.

Alex stopped stiffly a moment. Then, thinking steadiness would work best, he moved on.

The horse stirred restlessly, but not much: a few heavy steps away, a few back closer.

Alex moved closer. He could see the coarse fuzz of the winter hair. It made the horse look orange-colored. He kept moving closer. The horse ambled slowly away from the gate, turned its rump toward him, then stood eyeing him back around one shoulder. In spite of the thick hair, as it had moved, Alex had seen the rippling of ribs. His hopes rose higher; everything—the ribbiness, the stirring about minus any crowhops or short quick dashes, the bony thrusts of the hips and withers—all spoke of age and a bigger chance of gentleness.

Then the horse broke away and in a slow, jolting trot curved wide around him, swinging back into the wind over a hundred yards away, and stopped, with her forelegs wide, and her head stretching cautiously down to sniff at the trail he'd made. The trot had pleased Alex for he'd seen by the smooth belly line that the horse was a mare. And now she seemed calmed by the man scent she was finding. She only stood with her head up and stared. A brown horse; solid brown, blurred by an orange fuzz.

Alex stared back, equally baffled, wondering what to do next. Then she started ambling toward him.

She stopped about thirty yards away. She looked him over. She saw none of the loose, thin ends that meant ropes or bridles, nor did she see or smell any buckets of grain. Alex started to bring out a handful of cut grass, and at that first motion she lunged away into a lope, which slowed into a trot as Morena headed upwind for the concealment of a draw, a quarter mile beyond, where she had sheltered through the night.

Alex saw her direction, and then glanced up the open slope, and seeing no sign of any vehicles, he began to follow. He began planning that with bluff and shout he might corner her there.

Morena reached the draw well in the lead, but swerved away from reentering the deeper snow. She put her trust in open distance, and again trotted in a wide curve around the man, and was disappointed to find that the gate had not been left open behind him. When the man started back toward her, the message was clear: she was being chased.

Alex had gotten a message, too. "She wants out of here as bad as I do," he said to his other self that suddenly seemed to be there with him. "We could get out of here together, easy, if she weren't so trotting dumb!" he complained.

"Easy now, you're just starting," said the other self.

The gray morning was becoming brighter, a gray brightness beneath the clouds, and even a bit warmer. Again Alex looked upslope to where the road ought to lie, lightly hidden by the snow, and he looked off southward across the slopes toward where, last night, the buses' lights had gone winking away.

He felt a tinge of worry that he saw no movements, except for puffs of snow flurried up by the wind. But he told himself a plow would move slowly; they'd probably have to come behind a plow. And maybe the low clouds were still snowing down on the plains, or the wind had left deeper drifts there. Actually, it was probably still early.

He dug out two pocketfuls of the fresh-cut grass and went toward the mare, offering the thick handful ahead of him.

Morena understood the offering and jogged away. Nearly always through her long life, food offered close by a man meant getting caught, and getting caught had meant more work than food.

But again she didn't run off far. She wasn't too nervous when she couldn't be caught, and she knew that men on foot couldn't catch her in the open. She trotted around the man again, then went loping past the gate again.

"Keep after her," urged Alex's inner self. "Don't let her get away with that. Wear her down."

Alex tried staying slowly and steadily behind her; he tried talking low and soothing to her, though his voice, out in the open, sounded awfully small and weak. The mare simply paced away from him.

She never went far. Morena was hungry. She already sensed the newly rising air pressure that spoke of a clear and bitterly cold night ahead. She knew that beyond the gate she could work her way lower and lower to more feed and warmth.

Now Alex was jogging after her, trying to cut across her circles, trying with waves of his arms to crowd her against the straight fence, trying just by doggedness to will her down. Sometimes he got close enough to hear her insides jiggling. He took off his handkerchief—maybe that was spooking her.

The haystacks she knew of, the frigid night she expected; these were just vaguenesses in her mind. The man was real and nearby. So Morena made no compromise. She would not give up her freedom to get through the gate.

Alex's own empty stomach began to gnaw and drag at him. The grass he'd cut became an aggravation. He couldn't throw it or shoot it. He just had to hold it out and beg. The continuing lack of success weighed him down. He quit.

Paul Zachary Cohen

Then that inner self mocked him: "Time goes slow when you just stand around waiting. You don't reckon you're not good enough to catch her, do you?"

"Look," he said. "If I'm going to do all this moving around I might as well find that road and start down it."

"You can't make thirty miles, not through fresh snow. It's probably fifteen to a ranch, if you can find one."

"I won't have to; they'll be coming to meet me."

"Okay, if you want to get rescued. Me. I'd rather be making my own way, and only get helped."

The idea stirred him. It was early, and warmth was rising with the daylight. He was sure someone would be coming before long. In fact, there'd be lots of people searching for him. The whole countryside would be out to help Alex Jaynes home. And the questions would start: Why'd you let it happen? Why weren't you better dressed? Why didn't you have any matches? Sure, he'd gotten through the night by himself, but it'd be better not to be just waiting helplessly. Getting stranded without matches or food or enough clothing bothered him too, just thinking about it, without lots of people asking him questions to make him look like some kind of infant.

He wanted to joke about his mistakes. If he had that horse and was making his own way, then he could laugh with them. He'd be as good as anyone who met him.

He looked nervously across the long white slopes hoping not to see anything, not yet. He wanted to catch the horse and be safe and riding her before they reached him.

"Move!—Dammit!—"

Unrushed, but steadily, red leaked out from the orange

in the sky and spread and formed streaks of its own. Unrushed, but steadily, pale greens and blues washed in from the west and deepened and fanned.

"Dammit!—Do it right!—"

Unrushed, but steadily, the sky seemed almost to laugh, a clownish face peering down, smeared with glowing colors. Unrushed, but steadily, red and yellows thinned and weakened; the greens shrank upward deep into blues.

"Please!—Move!—Please!"

Unrushed, but steadily, the blues turned to rich purple, then faltered, and grew dull. The sky was gray. A few tiny stars appeared, glittering clearly.

But Alex didn't reach for his knife. "Just one more time," he grunted, and grunted again, and finally she reacted in the right way; she cramped the trapped leg away from the lifted limb and dragged herself free and heaved shakily up on her hooves. He stumbled awkwardly toward her, on cold feet. She was too stiffened to get away. She didn't try. He caught her and stood with his arm hooked through the belt around her neck and pressed his paining fingers into the warmth beneath her mane. For his feet there was no relief but to stamp them up and down. His shoulders kept wanting to shiver, but that was as much from the relief of getting her loose as from the cold. His thoughts soared with the *un*-panicky feeling that he was winning. He was going to make it!

Morena stood holding one hind leg off the ground; not the leg that was pinned, but the other, the left one. She accepted the man's steady hold around her neck. She was used to that kind of control. Her energies had been drained for the moment. It was one more of those rare moments that she felt a man's presence as soothing.

Alex was amazed at how untired and unsleepy he felt. His head worked sharp and clear. He saw there was no point in getting on her now: she couldn't carry him up the embankment, and the brush surrounding them was too thick to ride through. He'd have to mount when he got in the open—but, at last, he knew how. So first he led her slowly about the deep twilight in the hollow of the draw's bottom; it was all a cold stillness of snow grays and brush blacks. She limped, favoring a hind foot.

"Got yourself pinched, did you?" he said gently. "It'll loosen up with walking," he promised. He moved around till he found a long, thin forked branch he could break off. Then he broke off an arm of the branch so that he had a piece of wood shaped like a long checkmark. With the hook of the check through the belt he could reach her tail and still have hold of her.

He began slicing off long strands of hair. Several times he had to stop and warm his fingers against her body; he wished he knew how to warm his toes, too. He twisted strands of tail hair into long bunches that he tied into loops, one through the other, making a daisy-chain. When he got ready to tie an end loop to a knot in her mane, he'd have a ladder to climb on with.

He put the loops inside his shirt so the brush wouldn't snag them, and began trying to get up on open pasture. "Come on, old girl," he said.

The light breeze greeted them there; light, but singeing with chill. Alex connected his horsehair chain, abandoned his checkmark stick, and while she kept turning toward him, he climbed up and aboard.

"Atta girl. Atta girl," he murmured to her when he was seated. He had to lean way forward on her neck to keep hold of the belt, so he undid the top loop of tail hair and tied it to the belt. Now he had a rein, all of one he should need. It was simple. He couldn't understand why he hadn't thought of it before. All her extra strength and speed was now his, and it felt tremendous.

He lightly urged her into motion, letting her pick the way. She seemed ready to head toward someplace, probably to shelter. The earth was aglow with snowlight. The sky was black and glittering with stars. The directions were clear. She was heading east, toward the highway. She kept limping, still favoring the hind foot. "It'll get warmed up and feeling better," he encouraged her. "The best thing's to keep it moving—old friend."

Low in front of him he saw a star moving. Then another. In fact, there were three of them, spaced out and moving, very slowly; and one more moving the other way. Headlights, he recognized. He was seeing the highway, maybe not much more than twenty miles, direct from where he was.

Her bony spine was gouging hard between his hips, but he didn't mind; he clung close to her warm, solid, hairy strength. It was his safety. The prize he'd won. And he knew for sure why it was he hadn't let himself throw up in the bus, or stay shivering close to the roadway, or cut her throat in the draw and crouch down hoping the cold wouldn't find him. He didn't want to have to accept anyone's forgiveness for stinking up their air, or bringing them out in the cold. Because it seemed like a part of you died and was lost, anyway, every time you did that. He wanted to do things on his own, get there on his own. He was as good as the chickadees. As big as the horse. He'd never felt freer and more whole than he did at that moment.

He grinned down at them, those people hunched in their cars, crowded up close to the heaters they needed, and not knowing they were being watched, not knowing what was going on in the rugged world around them. But he was surviving this world they were hurrying to be shielded from, and he was going down to show them.

"They can't desert us, can they, horse. We'll show 'em."

Morena's hind foot pained her if she stepped on it. It didn't bother her if she held it up, but it was difficult to gimp through the snow on three feet, and she had to keep setting it down again and again. She wanted to stop. But the will of a man on her back had always proved irresistibly strong, and she had learned early to obey it. And her hunger urged her on toward the haystacks. But Morena had little pride when other horses were not around, and it would have taken much pride to dull the stabbing in her hind foot, and to soften and freshen the stiff age in her muscles; much pride to make her try to move smoothly and gamely. She *hobbled*. Eventually she reached another fence line, right at a gateway. The gate was open and she started through, but the rider made her stop.

The fence line offered a hitching post, should he need it, yet Alex just sat, knowing that the limp was getting worse and that he shouldn't ignore it. But he didn't want to get off the horse.

He wondered if she were faking. He knew that if something was caught in her hoof, and stayed there, she could lame up and move too slow to get anywhere. The snow beginning to squeak beneath her steps left no doubt that the rigid cold was settling. His feet were numb beneath the grip of his knees against her ribs. His feet would be warmer moving about in the snow than dangling in the air. He might save his hands under her mane but his feet and ears could freeze if he had to ride too long. He knew he ought to get down for a while anyway. He could get up again easy now.

Slowly, he slid off of her. He gathered his rein of loops loosely in his hand, and shoved his hands in his pocket. He stood hunched and shivering, and not eager to try wrestling with the hoof she was holding up. But he was again suddenly aware of how small each step of his own would be compared to the brittle snow-gray world all around him. He didn't know where any shelter was. He'd have to ride, and ride at a trot in order to get anywhere in time. A trot bareback was jolting, but it got you warm. He looked closely at the hind leg she was favoring. He told himself he'd gotten this far, so he was tough enough to handle it.

64

And the tiny headlights slowly moving in the silent distance reminded him of who he was and where he would finally have to go. He wasn't going to have to make any excuses for coming in on a crippled horse.

He tied his rein to the fence's brace post, then stepped back to lay a palm on the bunched-up hip above the leg she was favoring. "Easy now, girl," he spoke to her, and heard his jaw only able to mumble again from the cold. But it didn't worry him; it didn't count now. "I gotta see what's here." He let his hand travel smoothly down the leg. It was a risky business picking up some horses' feet. He didn't want to get slammed and broken now. But she was old. "Easy now," he kept talking. "Easy. I bet you've had your hooves picked up and trimmed a thousand times."

He crouched in close beside her, knowing it was safer to be near the start of a kick than near the end of it. He took a deep breath, exhaled another. "Easy girl." He reached down and took hold of the feathering of hair just behind the hoof and tugged it forward and upward a little. He clamped his thighs together and got the front of the hoof resting against the sloping platform on his lap. Then he learned she was used to this, too used to it: she leaned on him, and his feet pained with cold as part of her weight sank through his legs. The underside of the hoof was packed with snow. With one hand he reached his knife, and began to scrape the snow away. Only then did it occur to him that this wasn't the leg that'd been pinned, and he wondered if he was as alert as he thought he was.

He was alert enough to see the splinter of wood emerging from the snow. It was lodged in one of the "frog hollows"—the grooves around the fleshy T-shaped pad that cushioned the hoof's step. A reward from all that useless banging and kicking about. She was old, and the pad was thin and hard. He tried to dig the splinter out with his finger, but it was wedged and held by snow stamped to water and frozen again. The flesh of his finger began to freeze and tear first. Then his back began to quiver with the strain, and so he couldn't keep his knees from shaking, too, and he had to let go, and straighten up.

He panted, and moved stiffly about, shaking his feet, trying to get some bearable relief from their aching. Then he patted her flank and felt again, old and skinny though she was, how much bigger and solider she was than he.

"Easy again, now, girl," he murmured. "Easy." He ran his hand slowly down the ridge of her leg. Abruptly she jerked up, and he leaped away, and she jumped. For a moment both of them staggered about defensively, as Alex began to understand she hadn't been kicking, but merely lifting her leg for him.

"Easy, girl. Easy." He started again. He crouched down, and tugged, and gritted against the weight she abruptly shifted to him. He was scared of prying and suddenly pricking too deep with the clumsy, broken point of the knife, so he used the back of the blade and sharply struck to break the ice. It was like the tap of a shoer's hammer. A sharp, hard snap; a startling voice without a body or smell or meaning she ever felt sure of. It had always unnerved her. She swiftly drew up her leg and kicked blindly at it.

Alex felt the hoof jerk up past his shoulder, and as he tried to jump aside the leg kicked by him at a glance so hard that he was shoved into running faster than his own legs could move, and he unbalanced into a snowy roll.

The extra dim commotion made Morena more startled, and she kicked and crowhopped about in nervous alarm, still fighting the ghost with the sharp touch and voice. The horsehair holding her to the brace post snapped with the first jump and she moved willy-nilly out on the pasture, then realized she was free and moved on.

Alex tried to follow, at first slow and then running, as best he could in the snow. But she wouldn't let him close, and even on three legs she could go faster than he when she had to. Soon it was hard just to see her in the darkness, even against the dull white sweep of the snow.

Only the stars were clear, and the little lights on the highway, and the squeaking of the snow. The scuffed trail she'd left in the snow was difficult to follow, for the snow broke too softly to shadow well, but he kept finding it, following it.

He put his knife away when the cold ache in one hand told him he still carried it. He wondered why he hadn't fallen on it. He certainly hadn't thought to throw it out of his way. No, he wasn't as alert as he should be. But now he still had it. He wondered why. He didn't want to believe it was luck. If he hadn't stabbed himself just because of luck, he'd have to thank luck for whatever else he ever did. Then he thought of how an eyelid closed automatically when something got near the eye, and he decided he must have, that quick, without knowing it, held the knife flat. He didn't let his thoughts come to the main fact, that now he was without a horse or solid shelter. That thought would end everything, except the icy pains.

He began to wonder if he were in the grip of some Power, or God, like they spoke of in church. That idea made everything seem less threatening, in fact, interesting. He'd just have to keep going to find out how this mysterious Plan would all work out.

The thought of God had made him naturally glance upward. He saw the two Dippers curved in front of him: the horse's trail had turned northward. Yes, the distant headlights were off to his right. It didn't matter. The highway was too far off to reach afoot. The stars told him he'd gotten to ride less than an hour. It must be close to seven o'clock. There would be an hour more at the most, and then he'd begin to feel his feet and hands starting to puff and stiffen and die. He would get very sleepy. They said when you froze to death, you simply got pleasantly drowsy and drowsier.

Paul Zachary Cohen

If he'd turn back south, he might cut across the road from the campground, a lot sooner than he could reach the highway. But there was no one looking for him there anyway. He wasn't angry at them anymore for not being there. They probably had their reasons. He wasn't even angry at the horse; she'd gotten away, and in her place he'd probably have done the same thing. He just wanted to get where he wanted to get, that was all. He began to wonder if she were real, or just a dream, or a ghost leading him on. She seemed to be heading somewhere. East and north. To shelter? Anyway, his feet were a little warmer walking steadily than riding, and the breeze got to him less than when he was on the horse.

It occurred to Alex that if he didn't keep pumping along, the breeze would wipe out the trail ahead of him. But he was getting tired. And sleepy. He couldn't get worried or angry about that, either. He just had to keep going, no faster than was comfortable. Yet he started finding that the harder it was, the harder he kept wanting the going to be. He kept wanting to take and give as much as he could. They'd have a hard time finding him, even if they wanted to. The breeze was wiping out his trail, too. So he kept struggling, stumbling, north and east. He was going to make it on his own. Or become a mystery. And that was the next best thing.

SPURS FOR ANTONIA

K. W. EYRE

Down at the barn, the milk cows were beginning to stir and rustle in the sweet-smelling hay. Manuela's black hens were pulling their heads out from under their wings, but at the ranch house everyone was still asleep when Romero opened the kitchen door and tiptoed clumsily across the floor. He lighted the lamp on the shelf above the sink and looked quickly at the woodbox.

Good! Full to the top with oak chunks and fine dry kindling. A hot blaze under the frying pan and coffee pot would be only a matter of seconds. Breakfast would be ready in a wink, in spite of Manuela's scoffing boast that she was the only one on the ranch who could cook a respectable meal. Better walk softly! She would take a rolling pin to him if he spoiled her sleep, that fat, lazy sister of his!

Coffee, eggs, warmed-over *tortillas,* and honey to spread on them, amber brown, from the hives in Sage Canyon. Romero nodded with satisfaction, and licked his sticky fingers as he set the waxy honeycomb on the table and poured milk in a glass. His little Tonita liked milk when the cream floated on top, thick and lumpy. While he smiled affectionately, thinking about her, the hall door opened and Antonia ran in with an excited, whispered good morning.

"Buenas dias! Am I on time, Romero? I was scared the

clock wouldn't go off! Manuela's still asleep. She didn't hear a thing, even when my boots dropped on the floor!''

She giggled, at the thought of Manuela deep in her blankets, and sitting down at the table she began to eat as fast as she could get her fork to her mouth.

Spring roundup time had come at last. Though it was only four o'clock and still dark, she and Romero would soon be riding out of the corral to catch up with her father and the Aguas Vivas outfit. The boss had been in the hills with his *vaqueros* for more than a week, rounding up the four thousand head of cattle that were scattered from the wide oak-shaded valleys of the flatlands to the rough, brushy wild country that lay far to the north and west, almost in sound of the sea.

Antonia sighed blissfully, thinking of the day ahead. Only a few short months ago she had never even been on a horse. She had never done anything more exciting than take stupid walks along prim streets with Great Aunt Alicia; nothing more interesting than sitting in the parlor on winter afternoons, close to the stuffy little coal grate, her face burning hot as she learned to stitch wool roses on a piece of scratchy canvas. And now, today, she and Lucky were going to be part of a rodeo!

When breakfast was over and the kitchen left tidy enough to meet Manuela's sharp eyes, Antonia and Romero saddled their horses and rode out of the corral. With a quick slap of her knotted reins on Lucky's flanks, Antonia hurried ahead to swing open the wide heavy gate.

"I can do it myself," she insisted importantly, leaning out of the saddle and struggling with the bars. "You don't have to help me at all." Romero's black eyes under their scraggly brows were bright with approval as she sidled her horse handily against the gate and made him stand quietly while she dropped the wire loop over the fence post.

The grass was high against their stirrups as they took the river trail. After the long late rains the feed had grown magically, tall and sweet and full of strength, and Antonia knew, confidently and happily, that a good year lay ahead for the boss of the Aguas Vivas rancho. A good year for the Sloane family, too. No doubt, now, about those long pants for Joe.

Humming a contented, wordless little song, she let Lucky carry her along through the poppies and purple lupine, his head tossing in time with the quick step of his newly shod hoofs and the jingle of bit and bridle. A smart cow pony knew what to expect on a fine spring morning like this. When the long line of bawling, white-faced cattle wound off the hills with the Aguas Vivas outfit riding herd behind them, he would have his eager, sweating, flying-hoofed share in the important business of driving them to the holding corrals to wait their turn for parting out and vaccination and branding.

"How much longer will the rodeo last, Romero?" Antonia asked, leaning out of the saddle to pick a yellow poppy for her hatband. "Till the end of the week?"

"Yes," the old *Californio* answered, "and don't forget, Tonita, when the hard work is over, when the *riatas* have been thrown in the last loops, when the branding irons have cooled, then will come the barbecue down by the willows."

"Will it be fun?"

"More than you can imagine, *amigacita*," Romero nodded, his eyes sparkling. "This year, because you have brought us luck, because the grass is high, your father has invited all the neighbors. There will be steaks from a fat steer, and *frijoles* to feed a hundred people! The *patrón* considers it proper that the countryside meet his daughter."

"I can't wait! Will you play your guitar, Romero? Will you sing, the way you do down at the bunk house? We can hear you, every night after supper. Pops likes the song about the jumping flea, but I like the one about the star, best."

"Estrellita? Si, that is a song you shall have at the barbecue, I promise."

Two hours later Antonia reined in Lucky and looked

anxiously along the high ridge that led to Moon Valley. "Isn't this where Pops said to wait, Romero? You don't think he could have driven the cattle around the other way? I'd hate to miss anything." Her face clouded as she spoke, and her gray eyes were sulky. "I wish I could have gone along and stayed all week with him! Camping out would be wonderful. Joe went—I don't see why I couldn't!"

Romero raised his eyebrows. "Oh, so life is very hard for you, my little *tecolote*? You think things are not fair?"

Antonia's face reddened. "Well, just the same, if I were a boy, like Joe, I'd be lucky. I could ride right alongside of Pops. He'd teach me to rope! He'd let me practice on the calves! He wouldn't say, 'No, you can't have a *riata* to throw, you might get a finger pulled off.'"

She looked down resentfully at her small sun-browned hands, and then went on in a burst of self-pity, "I'd get a chance to sleep out on the hills, with the stars right on top of my head! Joe says you can reach up and touch them. He says here on the ranch they're bigger and brighter and closer than anywhere else in the whole world."

Romero shook his head, his eyes wise and kind. "Poor Tonita *mia*! Fighting so hard against the way God made you! Tell me, to be a boy, is that truly so fine a thing? No, no, little one! Be patient. When the right time comes, you will ride every year to the roundup with *el patrón*. But now you are only a small one, and rodeos are for men." He sighed and smiled as he looked down at the little, slim, straight-backed girl riding next to him.

"Remember, Tonita, what I once told you? That poor old Romero would have nothing to do all day but sit in the sun and dream the hours away if your legs grew too long—if your eyes too wise? Be kind to me, *amiga*! Do not grow up too fast. Let me ride by your side for a long time to come."

Antonia stared at him. "Why, of course, we'll always ride together. Always and always!"

Romero smiled again, gravely. "Every day, Tonita *mia*, until the last leaf is blown from the tree. But now, we

74

have talked enough, you think? Let us ride fast, *vaquero*. The cattle will top the ridge in another half hour.''

He touched Pronto with his spurs and, as the big gray horse shot ahead, Antonia slapped the sorrel on his red rump, and they circled out into a wide loop that would bring them to the rear of the oncoming cattle's downhill swing. Antonia suddenly pulled up with an excited shout. ''There they are!''

Sitting straight and eager in her saddle, she waved her hat wildly as the vanguard of the great lurching, pushing, bellowing herd topped the ridge and wound down the trail in an unending line.

Shading her eyes against the glare, she stared impatiently. Oh, there was Pops! And there was Mr. Sloane, riding his bay colt. What a beauty! Look at it dance! When Mr. Sloane got through breaking it, when there was a real bit in its mouth instead of a hackamore around its nose, you would see a fine cow horse, almost as good as any in Pops's string. And look—there was Joe, following along on Whitey.

''Hi, Joe—did you have a good time?'' Antonia's excited greeting was lost in the pound of horses' hoofs and the bawling, grunting rush of cattle, as the outfit, yelling and hallooing, herded the cows and calves down the steep trail. Joe grinned through the dust and sweat on his face and waved his hat as he galloped past.

''Hi, Tony! You sure missed it, not comin' along. Oh boy!'' Antonia glanced at Romero out of the corner of her eye, and then she shouted to Joe, with her nose in the air, ''Camping isn't so much; I'd rather ride with Romero any day!'' She dug her heels into Lucky then, and rode forward to meet her father, her yellow head high.

The boss, unshaven and grimy, his eyes bloodshot from sun and wind and dust, smiled as she loped next to him. ''Good work, cowpuncher—you must have started early to catch up with us. I've got a job ready for you. Want to ride along while I bring in those yearling calves up there in that gulch—see, up there to the left, in the brush? They think they're hiding out on us, the little devils! Well, when we get them rounded up, we'll be through for the day. The men won't be sorry, and neither will I. It's been a tough week.'' He pulled a handkerchief out of his pocket and wiped the sweat that stood in beads on his forehead and blinked the dust from his strained tired eyes.

Then, while Antonia stared open-mouthed, he gave a quick exclamation, spurred Chavez abruptly, and whirled his horse down the trail at top speed. Oh! Oh! The colt! Bucking wildly, Mr. Sloane's young green horse was lunging through the cattle, scattering them in every direction as he reared and snorted and whirled.

The bellow of four hundred terrified animals, and the din of cowboy yells told the tale. By the time Joe's father got his bay colt gentled down, the herd would be spread from here to China! While she stared horrified, Romero wheeled past her, galloping at top speed, with Joe close behind spurring Whitey.

All along the line, the outfit closed in, shouting, and yelling and prodding. Completely bewildered by the sudden confusion, her heart pounding hard, Antonia hung on to the reins and tried her best to quiet Lucky's excited prancing. What was the best thing to do, when you found yourself alone on a hillside, with outfit and cattle floundering down below you in a choking cloud of dust? One thing was sure—you had sense enough to keep out of the way. Nobody wanted a girl around when four hundred cattle were on the rampage. She would just have to sit and wait until the excitement died down. It would be at least an hour before anyone got around to giving her the slightest thought.

She stared down the trail, coughing away the gritty dust that burned her throat and hanging on to the reins as tight as she could. Maybe Lucky wouldn't jump around so much, maybe he wouldn't pull so hard, if he had something interesting to do—if his mind were taken off that milling, bawling mixup down below. What was it her father had said about a little bunch of calves up there on the side hill, in the brush? Why, of course! It would help a lot if she brought them down and headed them toward the holding corral. Poor Pops. He was so tired already that he would be glad to have the job done for him. This was a chance to help.

Reining Lucky toward the brushy gulch that split a deep gash in the hillside, Antonia took the trail that climbed steeply through yellow mustard and tall grass. Far below she could hear the outfit shouting as they rode hard on the heels of the scattered herd and, turning in the saddle, she saw the dim shapes of cattle and horses moving through the brown dust of the river flat.

Now, what would be the first thing to do? How should she go about the business of rounding up those yearling calves? Perhaps she could not manage it all alone, but at least she could try. Without practice, no one could expect to turn into a real *vaquero*. What a golden opportunity!

She let Lucky stop for a breathing spell and began to count the calves that were huddled ahead of her, under the shelter of a scrub oak thicket. Ten of them. They needn't think they could hide. Didn't they know that the boss wanted them at the corrals? And that was where they were going.

She snatched off her hat and waved it wildly as she kicked her heels into the sorrel and sent him along the trail on a run. "Get going, Lucky boy! Yahoo—yipee! Yahoo!" In sturdy imitation of Joe Sloane's cowboy yells, Antonia shouted at the top of her lungs. "Atta boy, Lucky! Chase 'em out of there! Yahoo! Yipee!" The white-faced yearlings fixed astonished eyes on her for a moment, and then turned and broke into a run for the thick brush.

The grass and the mustard stalks had disappeared now, and rough sage and chaparral scratched Antonia's face and arms as she ducked from thicket to thicket, trying to be in ten places at once. The calves thoroughly understood that this business of being a *vaquero* was something quite new to her. Here and there, everywhere, they ran from one brushy cover to another.

No sooner did Lucky have them covered and headed downhill, than they broke away and scattered again in ten separate directions. The little sorrel did his best. Gallantly he worked with all the heart and intelligence of a seasoned cow horse. This way and that he turned, with Antonia half out of the saddle as he whirled to head off a calf. With her yellow hair blowing in streamers, she jammed her sombrero down over her ears and caught her breath grimly.

Grabbing the horn of the saddle, she held on for dear life. Pulling leather was a big help—as long as no one was around to see you. Whew—Joe would have to admit that Lucky could turn on a dime! She clenched her blue-jeaned legs against the sorrel's sweating flanks and laughed aloud, half frightened to death, half crazy with glorious excitement.

If she could only hang on long enough, she and Lucky would have those calves just where they wanted them! Pops and the outfit, way, way down below, looked like little black ants. There wasn't time to notice how they were getting along. She had troubles of her own. Things were looking better, though—if she could only manage to circle around that pesky scrub oak and keep the calves on the run. Good old Lucky boy. Beautiful, darling Lucky. There wasn't a horse in the whole world who knew more about working cattle.

At last, one by one, the calves gave up their losing fight for freedom and dropped into line along the trail that led to the holding corrals and the river. Lucky kept close to their heels. The sorrel horse was not taking any chances, and at the first sign of bolting, he was off again at a run, heading them back with a quick turn, or a lightning jump that would throw Antonia out of the saddle onto his neck with squeals of surprise, and small, choked-back gasps of fright.

K. W. Eyre

"It's all right with me, Lucky, whatever you want to
do," she giggled meekly, her hands aching from their grip
on the reins, her knees rubbed sore as they clamped desperately. "You know lots more about roundups than I do."

When at last the steep narrow trail lay behind them, and
the flat, oak-dotted fields stretched ahead, Antonia, with a
tremendous, panting sigh of relief, took off her hat and
wiped the perspiration from her forehead. The worst was
over. The calves could see the other cattle ahead of them
now, and they could smell the river. They would not try to
break back to the brushy gulch again. All they wanted was
to run to the willows and join the herd that was wallowing
and snuffing and bellowing in the cool deep stream.

At the gate of the holding corral, meanwhile, the boss
turned to Romero with an anxious frown. "What do you
suppose is keeping Antonia? I lost track of her in all the
excitement, but I took for granted she was riding right behind us. I knew she'd have sense enough to keep out of the
way. Do you suppose she circled back and rode on home?"

Romero shook his head, his black eyes worried. "She
was on the hillside safely, holding Lucky quiet, *señor*,
when I looked back the last time to make sure all was well.
Because the little sorrel is so gentle, because he has a head
full of sense, I was not afraid to leave her alone. But now, if
you have no more need of me, *patrón*, Pronto and I will ride
back and look for her."

Joe Sloane, perched on top of the fence rail where he
had climbed while Whitey had a rest and a drink, broke into
the conversation, his blue eyes popping. "Guess you don't
have to worry about Tony any longer, boss. Take a look at
what's heading across the field, sir! The crazy kid—I'll be
doggoned!"

Almost knocked off the fence by surprise, Joe pointed,
his jaw dropping open. By golly! The Boston Bean herself,
ridin' herd on ten yearlin' calves, and that little ol' sorrel of
hers holdin' 'em in line like a veteran. The darn little

80

cayuse—look at him lope along—and look at that half-pint in the saddle, sittin' there as uppity and cool as all getout! Talk about your old timers! A fella could sure spot the makin's of a real cowhand when he saw one!

Mr. Rawlins, speechless, stared unbelievingly at the dusty, hot, disheveled little rider astride her sweat-stained horse, and Romero nudged him, chuckling and beaming, his eyes shining with pride. "*Si, señor*, it is truly our Tonita. You like a little yellow-head *vaquero* on the Aguas Vivas better than a mortgage, eh? I agree, *patrōn*!"

Joe, still gawking, scrambled off the fence and untied Whitey from the rails. Hallooing at the top of his lungs, he galloped off across the field to open the lower gate of the holding corral, and Antonia and Lucky drove their calves through to the riverbank and watched them lurch over the side into the water.

Antonia took off her hat again and fanned herself breathlessly, the noonday sun beating hotly on her tangled hair and on her dirty face. Her black eyelashes were gray with dust, and her blue cotton shirt was ripped on the right side in a long, brush-torn slit, from shoulder to cuff. From her right eye to her chin a jagged red scratch made a bright path through the dust and perspiration.

The boss, spurring Chavez, rode alongside of her and put out his big hand, his eyes warm with approval and pride.

"Shake, cowpuncher! You handled those cattle like a top hand. The outfit says you're hired! You've moved right in! But tell me something—whatever made you chase up the canyon after those yearlings, Antonia? What put the idea in your head?"

Antonia, with her grimy small hand in his, looked up at her father with surprised eyes.

"Well," she said simply, "you said you had a job for me. You said you wanted them in the corral, didn't you, Pops?"

THE GIFT

JOHN STEINBECK

(from *The Red Pony*)

AT daybreak Billy Buck emerged from the bunkhouse and stood for a moment on the porch looking up at the sky. He was a broad, bandy-legged little man with a walrus mustache, with square hands, puffed and muscled on the palms. His eyes were a contemplative, watery gray, and the hair which protruded from under his Stetson hat was spiky and weathered. Billy was still stuffing his shirt into his blue jeans as he stood on the porch. He unbuckled his belt and tightened it again. The belt showed, by the worn shiny places opposite each hole, the gradual increase of Billy's middle over a period of years. When he had seen to the weather, Billy cleared each nostril by holding its mate closed with his forefinger and blowing fiercely. Then he walked down to the barn, rubbing his hands together. He curried and brushed two saddle horses in the stalls, talking quietly to them all the time; and he had hardly finished when the iron triangle started ringing at the ranch house. Billy stuck the brush and currycomb together and laid them on the rail, and went up to breakfast. His action had been so deliberate and yet so wasteless of time that he came to the house while Mrs. Tiflin was still ringing the triangle. She nodded her gray head to him and withdrew into the kitchen. Billy Buck sat down on the steps, because he was a cowhand, and it wouldn't be fitting that he should go first into the dining room. He heard Mr. Tiflin in the house, stamping his feet into his boots.

The high jangling note of the triangle put the boy Jody in motion. He was only a little boy, ten years old, with hair like dusty yellow grass and with shy, polite gray eyes, and with a mouth that worked when he thought. The triangle picked him up out of sleep. It didn't occur to him to disobey the harsh note. He never had: no one he knew ever had. He brushed the tangled hair out of his eyes and skinned his nightgown off. In a moment he was dressed—blue chambray shirt and overalls. It was late in the summer, so of course there were no shoes to bother with. In the kitchen he waited until his mother got from in front of the sink and went back to the stove. Then he washed himself and brushed back his wet hair with his fingers. His mother turned sharply on him as he left the sink. Jody looked shyly away.

"I've got to cut your hair before long," his mother said. "Breakfast's on the table. Go on in, so Billy can come."

Jody sat at the long table which was covered with white oilcloth washed through to the fabric in some places. The fried eggs lay in rows on their platter. Jody took three eggs on his plate and followed with three thick slices of crisp bacon. He carefully scraped a spot of blood from one of the egg yolks.

Billy Buck clumped in. "That won't hurt you," Bill explained. "That's only a sign the rooster leaves."

Jody's tall stern father came in then. Jody knew from the noise on the floor that he was wearing boots, but he looked under the table anyway, to make sure. His father turned off the oil lamp over the table, for plenty of morning light now came through the windows.

Jody did not ask where his father and Billy Buck were riding that day, but he wished he might go along. His father was a disciplinarian. Jody obeyed him in everything without questions of any kind. Now, Carl Tiflin sat down and reached for the egg platter.

"Got the cows ready to go, Billy?" he asked.

"In the lower corral," Billy said. "I could just as well take them in alone."

"Sure you could. But a man needs company. Besides, your throat gets pretty dry." Carl Tiflin was jovial this morning.

Jody's mother put her head in the door. "What time do you think to be back, Carl?"

"I can't tell. I've got to see some men in Salinas. Might be gone till dark."

The eggs and coffee and big biscuits disappeared rapidly. Jody followed the two men out of the house. He watched them mount their horses and drive six old milk cows out of the corral and start over the hill toward Salinas. They were going to sell the old cows to the butcher.

When they had disappeared over the crown of the ridge Jody walked up the hill in back of the house. The dogs trotted around the house corner, hunching their shoulders and grinning horribly with pleasure. Jody patted their heads—Doubletree Mutt with the big thick tail and yellow eyes, and Smasher, the shepherd, who had killed a coyote and lost an ear in doing it. Smasher's one good ear stood up higher than a collie's ear should. Billy Buck said that always happened. After the frenzied greeting the dogs lowered their noses to the ground in a businesslike way and went ahead, looking back now and then to make sure that the boy was coming. They walked up through the chicken yard and saw the quail eating with the chickens. Smasher chased the chickens a little to keep in practice in case there should ever be sheep to herd. Jody continued on through the large vegetable patch where the green corn was higher than his head. The cow-pumpkins were green and small yet. He went on to the sagebrush line where the cold spring ran out of its pipe and fell into a round wooden tub. He leaned over and drank close to the green mossy wood where the water tasted best. Then he turned and looked back on the ranch, on the low, whitewashed house girded with red geraniums, and on the long bunkhouse by the cypress tree where Billy Buck lived alone. Jody could see the great black kettle under the cypress tree. That was where the pigs were scalded. The sun was coming over the ridge now, glaring on the whitewash of the houses and barns, making the wet grass blaze softly. Behind him, in the tall sagebrush, the birds were scampering on the ground, making a great noise among the dry leaves; the squirrels piped shrilly on the side hills. Jody looked along at the farm buildings. He felt an uncertainty in the air, a feeling of change and of loss and of the gain of new and unfamiliar things. Over the hillside two big black buzzards sailed low to the ground, and their shadows slipped smoothly and quickly ahead of them. Some animal had died in the vicinity. Jody knew it. It might be a cow or it might be the remains of a rabbit. The buzzards overlooked nothing. Jody hated them as all decent things hate them, but they could not be hurt because they made away with carrion.

After a while the boy sauntered downhill again. The dogs had long ago given him up and gone into the brush to do things in their own way. Back through the vegetable garden he went, and he paused for a moment to smash a green muskmelon with his heel, but he was not happy about it. It was a bad thing to do, he knew perfectly well. He kicked dirt over the ruined melon to conceal it.

Back at the house his mother bent over his rough hands, inspecting his fingers and nails. It did little good to start him clean to school, for too many things could happen on the way. She sighed over the black cracks on his fingers, and then gave him his books and his lunch and started him on the mile walk to school. She noticed that his mouth was working a good deal this morning.

Jody started his journey. He filled his pockets with little pieces of white quartz that lay in the road, and every so often he took a shot at a bird or at some rabbit that had stayed sunning itself in the road too long. At the crossroads over the bridge he met two friends and the three of them walked to school together, making ridiculous strides and being rather silly. School had just opened two weeks before. There was still a spirit of revolt among the pupils.

It was four o'clock in the afternoon when Jody topped the hill and looked down on the ranch again. He looked for the saddle horses, but the corral was empty. His father was not back yet. He went slowly, then, toward the afternoon chores. At the ranch house, he found his mother sitting on the porch, mending socks.

"There's two doughnuts in the kitchen for you," she said. Jody slid to the kitchen and returned with half of one of the doughnuts already eaten and his mouth full. His mother asked him what he had learned in school that day, but she didn't listen to his doughnut-muffled answer. She interrupted, "Jody, tonight see you fill the woodbox clear full. Last night you crossed the sticks and it wasn't only about half full. Lay the sticks flat tonight. And Jody, some of the hens are hiding eggs, or else the dogs are eating them. Look about in the grass and see if you can find any nests."

Jody, still eating, went out and did his chores. He saw the quail come down to eat with the chickens when he threw out the grain. For some reason his father was proud to have them come. He never allowed any shooting near the house for fear the quail might go away.

When the woodbox was full, Jody took his twenty-two rifle up to the cold spring at the brush line. He drank again and then aimed the gun at all manner of things, at rocks, at birds on the wing, at the big black pig-kettle under the cypress tree; he didn't shoot, for he had no cartridges and wouldn't have until he was twelve. If his father had seen him aim the rifle in the direction of the house he would have put the cartridges off another year. Jody remembered this and did not point the rifle down the hill again. Two years was enough to wait for cartridges. Nearly all of his father's presents were given with reservations which hampered their value somewhat. It was good discipline.

The supper waited until dark for his father to return. When at last he came in with Billy Buck, Jody could smell the delicious brandy on their breaths. Inwardly he rejoiced, for his father sometimes talked to him when he smelled of brandy, sometimes even told things he had done in the wild days when he was a boy.

After supper, Jody sat by the fireplace and his shy polite eyes sought the room corners, and he waited for his father to tell what it was he contained, for Jody knew he had news of some sort. But he was disappointed. His father pointed a stern finger at him.

"You'd better go to bed, Jody. I'm going to need you in the morning."

That wasn't so bad. Jody liked to do the things he had to do as long as they weren't routine things. He looked at the floor and his mouth worked out a question before he spoke it, "What are we going to do in the morning, kill a pig?" he asked softly.

"Never you mind. You better get to bed."

When the door closed behind him, Jody heard his father and Billy Buck chuckling and he knew it was a joke of some kind. And later, when he lay in bed, trying to make words out of the murmurs in the other room, he heard his father protest, "But, Ruth, I didn't give much for him."

Jody heard the hoot owls hunting mice down by the barn, and he heard a fruit tree limb tap-tapping against the house. A cow was lowing when he went to sleep.

When the triangle sounded in the morning, Jody dressed more quickly even than usual. In the kitchen, while he washed his face and combed back his hair, his mother addressed him irritably. "Don't you go out until you get a good breakfast in you."

He went into the dining room and sat at the long white table. He took a steaming hotcake from the platter, arranged two fried eggs on it, covered them with another hotcake and squashed the whole thing with his fork.

His father and Billy Buck came in. Jody knew from the sound on the floor that both of them were wearing flat-heeled shoes, but he peered under the table to make sure. His father turned off the oil lamp, for the day had arrived, and he looked stern and disciplinary; but Billy Buck didn't look at Jody at all. He avoided the shy questioning eyes of the boy and soaked a whole piece of toast in his coffee.

Carl Tiflin said crossly, "You come with us after breakfast!"

Jody had trouble with his food then, for he felt a kind of doom in the air. After Billy had tilted his saucer and drained the coffee which had slopped into it, and had wiped his hands on his jeans, the two men stood up from the table and went out into the morning light together, and Jody respectfully followed a little behind them. He tried to keep his mind from running ahead, tried to keep it absolutely motionless.

His mother called, "Carl! Don't you let it keep him from school."

They marched past the cypress, where a singletree hung from a limb to butcher the pigs on, and past the black iron kettle, so it was not a pig-killing. The sun shone over the hill and threw long, dark shadows of the trees and buildings. They crossed a stubble field to short-cut to the barn. Jody's father unhooked the door and they went in. They had been walking toward the sun on the way down. The barn was black as night in contrast, and warm from the hay and from the beasts. Jody's father moved over toward the one box stall. "Come here!" he ordered. Jody could begin to see things now. He looked into the box stall and then stepped back quickly.

A red pony colt was looking at him out of the stall. Its tense ears were forward and a light of disobedience was in

its eyes. Its coat was rough and thick as an Airedale's fur and its mane was long and tangled. Jody's throat collapsed in on itself and cut his breath short.

"He needs a good currying," his father said, "and if I ever hear of you not feeding him or leaving his stall dirty, I'll sell him off in a minute."

Jody couldn't bear to look at the pony's eyes anymore. He gazed down at his hands for a moment, and he asked very shyly, "Mine?" No one answered him. He put his hand out toward the pony. Its gray nose came close, sniffing loudly, and then the lips drew back and the strong teeth closed on Jody's fingers. The pony shook its head up and down and seemed to laugh with amusement. Jody regarded his bruised fingers. "Well," he said with pride—"Well, I guess he can bite all right." The two men laughed, somewhat in relief. Carl Tiflin went out of the barn and walked up a side hill to be by himself, for he was embarrassed, but Billy Buck stayed. It was easier to talk to Billy Buck. Jody asked again—"Mine?"

Billy became professional in tone. "Sure! That is, if you look out for him and break him right. I'll show you how. He's just a colt. You can't ride him for some time."

Jody put out his bruised hand again, and this time the red pony let his nose be rubbed. "I ought to have a carrot," Jody said. "Where'd we get him, Billy?"

"Bought him at a sheriff's auction," Billy explained. "A show went broke in Salinas and had debts. The sheriff was selling off their stuff."

The pony stretched out his nose and shook the forelock from his wild eyes. Jody stroked the nose a little. He said softly, "There isn't a—saddle?"

Billy Buck laughed. "I'd forgot. Come along."

In the harness room he lifted down a little saddle of red morocco leather. "It's just a show saddle," Billy Buck said disparagingly. "It isn't practical for the brush, but it was cheap at the sale."

John Steinbeck

Jody couldn't trust himself to look at the saddle either, and he couldn't speak at all. He brushed the shining red leather with his fingertips, and after a long time he said, "It'll look pretty on him though." He thought of the grandest and prettiest things he knew. "If he hasn't a name already, I think I'll call him Gabilan Mountains," he said.

Billy Buck knew how he felt. "It's a pretty long name. Why don't you just call him Gabilan? That means hawk. That would be a fine name for him." Billy felt glad. "If you will collect tail hair, I might be able to make a hair rope for you sometime. You could use it for a hackamore."

Jody wanted to go back to the box stall. "Could I lead him to school, do you think—to show the kids?"

But Billy shook his head. "He's not even halter broke yet. We had a time getting him here. Had to almost drag him. You better be starting for school though."

"I'll bring the kids to see him here this afternoon," Jody said.

Six boys came over the hill half an hour early that afternoon, running hard, their heads down, their forearms working, their breath whistling. They swept by the house and cut across the stubble field to the barn. And then they stood selfconsciously before the pony, and then they looked at Jody with eyes in which there was a new admiration and a new respect. Before today Jody had been a boy dressed in overalls and a blue shirt, quieter than most, even suspected of being a little cowardly. And now he was different. Out of a thousand centuries they drew the ancient admiration of the footman for the horseman. They knew instinctively that a man on a horse is spiritually as well as physically bigger than a man on foot. They knew that Jody had been miraculously lifted out of equality with them and had been placed over them. Gabilan put his head out of the stall and sniffed them.

"Why'n't you ride him?" the boys cried. "Why'n't you braid his tail with ribbons like in the fair?" "When you going to ride him?"

Jody's courage was up. He too felt the superiority of the horseman. "He's not old enough. Nobody can ride him for a long time. I'm going to train him on the long halter. Billy Buck is going to show me how."

"Well, can't we even lead him around a little?"

"He isn't even halter broke," Jody said. He wanted to be completely alone when he took the pony out the first time. "Come and see the saddle."

They were speechless at the red morocco saddle, completely shocked out of comment. "It isn't much use in the brush," Jody explained. "It'll look pretty on him though. Maybe I'll ride bareback when I go into the brush."

"How you going to rope a cow without a saddle horn?"

"Maybe I'll get another saddle for everyday. My father might want me to help him with the stock." He let them feel the red saddle and showed them the brass chain throatlatch on the bridle and the big brass buttons at each temple where the headstall and brow band crossed. The whole thing was too wonderful. They had to go away after a little while, and each boy, in his mind, searched among his possessions for a bribe worthy of offering in return for a ride on the red pony when the time should come.

Jody was glad when they had gone. He took brush and currycomb from the wall, took down the barrier of the box stall and stepped cautiously in. The pony's eyes glittered, and he edged around into kicking position. But Jody touched him on the shoulder and rubbed his high arched neck as he had always seen Billy Buck do, and he crooned "so-o-o boy" in a deep voice. The pony gradually relaxed his tenseness. Jody curried and brushed until a pile of dead hair lay in the stall and until the pony's coat had taken on a deep red shine. Each time he finished he thought it might have been done better. He braided the mane into a dozen little pigtails, and he braided the forelock, and then he undid them and brushed the hair out straight again.

Jody did not hear his mother enter the barn. She was angry when she came, but when she looked in at the pony and at Jody working over him, she felt a curious pride rise up in her. "Have you forgot the woodbox?" she asked gently. "It's not far off from dark and there's not a stick of wood in the house, and the chickens aren't fed."

Jody quickly put up his tools. "I forgot, ma'am."

"Well, after this do your chores first. Then you won't forget. I expect you'll forget lots of things now if I don't keep an eye on you."

"Can I have carrots from the garden for him, ma'am?"

She had to think about that. "Oh—I guess so, if you only take the big tough ones."

"Carrots keep the coat good," he said, and again she felt the curious rush of pride.

Jody never waited for the triangle to get him out of bed after the coming of the pony. It became his habit to creep out of bed even before his mother was awake, to slip into his clothes and to go quietly down to the barn to see Gabilan. In the gray quiet mornings when the land and the brush and the houses and the trees were silver-gray and black like a photograph negative, he stole toward the barn, past the sleeping stones and the sleeping cypress tree. The turkeys, roosting in the tree out of coyotes' reach, clicked drowsily. The fields glowed with a gray frostlike light, and in the dew the tracks of rabbits and of field mice stood out sharply. The good dogs came stiffly out of their little houses, hackles up and deep growls in their throats. Then they caught Jody's scent, and their stiff tails rose up and waved a greeting—Doubletree Mutt with the big thick tail, and Smasher, the incipient shepherd—then went lazily back to their warm beds.

It was a strange time and a mysterious journey to Jody—an extension of a dream. When he first had the pony he liked to torture himself during the trip by thinking Gabilan would not be in his stall, and worse, would never have been there. And he had other delicious little self-induced pains. He thought how the rats had gnawed ragged holes in the red saddle, and how the mice had nibbled Gabilan's tail until it was stringy and thin. He usually ran the last little way to the barn. He unlatched the rusty hasp of the barn door and stepped in, and no matter how quietly he opened the door, Gabilan was always looking at him over the barrier of the box stall and Gabilan whinnied softly and stamped his front foot, and his eyes had big sparks of red fire in them like oakwood embers.

Sometimes, if the work horses were to be used that day, Jody found Billy Buck in the barn harnessing and currying. Billy stood with him and looked long at Gabilan and he told Jody a great many things about horses. He explained that they were terribly afraid for their feet, so that one must make a practice of lifting the legs and patting the hooves and ankles to remove their terror. He told Jody how horses love conversation. He must talk to the pony all the time and tell him the reasons for everything. Billy wasn't sure a horse could understand everything that was said to him, but it was impossible to say how much was understood. A horse never kicked up a fuss if someone he liked explained things to him. Billy could give examples, too. He had known, for instance, a horse nearly dead beat with fatigue to perk up when told it was only a little farther to his destination. And he had known a horse paralyzed with fright to come out of it when his rider told him what it was that was frightening him. While he talked in the mornings, Billy Buck cut twenty or thirty straws into neat three-inch lengths and stuck them into his hatband. Then, during the whole day, if he wanted to pick his teeth or merely to chew on something, he had only to reach up for one of them.

97

John Steinbeck

Jody listened carefully, for he knew and the whole country knew that Billy Buck was a fine hand with horses. Billy's own horse was a stringy cayuse with a hammer head, but he nearly always won the first prizes at the stock trials. Billy could rope a steer, take a double half-hitch about the horn with his riata, and dismount; and his horse would play the steer as an angler plays a fish, keeping a tight rope until the steer was down or beaten.

Every morning, after Jody had curried and brushed the pony, he let down the barrier of the stall, and Gabilan thrust past him and raced down the barn and into the corral. Around and around he galloped, and sometimes he jumped forward and landed on stiff legs. He stood quivering, stiff ears forward, eyes rolling so that the whites showed, pretending to be frightened. At last he walked snorting to the water trough and buried his nose in the water up to the nostrils. Jody was proud then, for he knew that was the way to judge a horse. Poor horses only touched their lips to the water, but a fine spirited beast put his whole nose and mouth under, and only left room to breathe.

Then Jody stood and watched the pony, and he saw things he had never noticed about any other horse; the sleek, sliding flank muscles and the cords of the buttocks, which flexed like a closing fist, and the shine the sun put on the red coat. Having seen horses all his life, Jody had never looked at them very closely before. But now he noticed the moving ears which gave expression and even inflection of expression to the face. The pony talked with his ears. You could tell exactly how he felt about everything by the way his ears pointed. Sometimes they were stiff and upright and sometimes lax and sagging. They went back when he was angry or fearful, and forward when he was anxious and curious and pleased; and their exact position indicated which emotion he had.

Billy Buck kept his word. In the early fall the training began. First there was the halter-breaking, and that was the hardest because it was the first thing. Jody held a carrot and coaxed and promised and pulled on the rope. The pony set his feet like a burro when he felt the strain. But before long he learned. Jody walked all over the ranch leading him. Gradually he took to dropping the rope until the pony followed him unled wherever he went.

And then came the training on the long halter. That was slower work. Jody stood in the middle of a circle, holding the long halter. He clucked with his tongue and the pony started to walk in a big circle, held in by the long rope. He clucked again to make the pony trot, and again to make him gallop. Around and around Gabilan went, thundering and enjoying it immensely. Then Jody called "whoa," and the pony stopped. It was not long until Gabilan was perfect at it. But in many ways he was a bad pony. He bit Jody in the pants and stomped on Jody's feet. Now and then his ears went back and he aimed a tremendous kick at the boy. Every time he did one of these bad things, Gabilan settled back and seemed to laugh to himself.

Billy Buck worked at the hair rope in the evenings before the fireplace. Jody collected tail hair in a bag, and he sat and watched Billy slowly constructing the rope, twisting a few hairs to make a string and rolling two strings together for a cord, and then braiding a number of cords to make the rope. Billy rolled the finished rope on the floor under his foot to make it round and hard.

The long halter work rapidly approached perfection. Jody's father, watching the pony stop and start and trot and gallop, was a little bothered by it.

"He's getting to be almost a trick pony," he complained. "I don't like trick horses. It takes all the—dignity out of a horse to make him do tricks. Why, a trick horse is kind of like an actor—no dignity, no character of his own." And his father said, "I guess you better be getting him used to the saddle pretty soon."

Jody rushed for the harness room. For some time he had

99

been riding the saddle on a sawhorse. He changed the stirrup length over and over, and could never get it just right. Sometimes, mounted on the sawhorse in the harness room, with collars and hames and tugs hung all about him, Jody rode out beyond the room. He carried his rifle across the pommel. He saw the fields go flying by, and he heard the beat of the galloping hoofs.

It was a ticklish job, saddling the pony for the first time. Gabilan hunched and reared and threw the saddle off before the cinch could be tightened. It had to be replaced again and again until at last the pony let it stay. And the cinching was difficult too. Day by day Jody tightened the girth a little more until at last the pony didn't mind the saddle at all.

Then there was the bridle. Billy explained how to use a stick of licorice for a bit until Gabilan was used to having something in his mouth. Billy explained, "Of course we could force-break him to everything, but he wouldn't be as good a horse if we did. He'd always be a little bit afraid, and he wouldn't mind because he wanted to."

The first time the pony wore the bridle he whipped his head about and worked his tongue against the bit until the blood oozed from the corners of his mouth. He tried to rub the headstall off on the manger. His ears pivoted about and his eyes turned red with fear and with general rambunctiousness. Jody rejoiced, for he knew that only a mean-souled horse does not resent training.

And Jody trembled when he thought of the time when he would first sit in the saddle. The pony would probably throw him off. There was no disgrace in that. The disgrace would come if he did not get right up and mount again. Sometimes he dreamed that he lay in the dirt and cried and couldn't make himself mount again. The shame of the dream lasted until the middle of the day.

Gabilan was growing fast. Already he had lost the long-leggedness of the colt; his mane was getting longer and blacker. Under the constant currying and brushing his coat lay as smooth and gleaming as orange-red lacquer. Jody oiled the hoofs and kept them carefully trimmed so they would not crack.

The hair rope was nearly finished. Jody's father gave him an old pair of spurs and bent in the side bars and cut down the strap and took up the chainlets until they fitted. And then one day Carl Tiflin said, "The pony's growing faster than I thought. I guess you can ride him by Thanksgiving. Think you can stick on?"

"I don't know," Jody said shyly. Thanksgiving was only three weeks off. He hoped it wouldn't rain, for rain would spot the red saddle.

Gabilan knew and liked Jody by now. He nickered when Jody came across the stubble field, and in the pasture he came running when his master whistled for him. There was always a carrot for him, every time.

Billy Buck gave him riding instructions over and over. "Now when you get up there, just grab tight with your knees and keep your hands away from the saddle, and if you get throwed, don't let that stop you. No matter how good a man is, there's always some horse can pitch him. You just climb up again before he gets to feeling smart about it. Pretty soon he won't throw you no more, and pretty soon he can't throw you no more. That's the way to do it."

"I hope it don't rain before," Jody said.

"Why not? Don't want to get throwed in the mud?"

That was partly it, and also he was afraid that in the flurry of bucking Gabilan might slip and fall on him and break his leg or his hip. He had seen that happen to men before, had seen how they writhed on the ground like squashed bugs, and he was afraid of it.

He practiced on the sawhorse how he would hold the reins in his left hand and a hat in his right hand. If he kept his hands thus busy, he couldn't grab the horn if he felt himself going off. He didn't like to think of what would happen if he did grab the horn. Perhaps his father and Billy Buck would never speak to him again, they would be so ashamed. The news would get about and his mother would be ashamed too. And in the schoolyard—it was too awful to contemplate.

He began putting his weight in a stirrup when Gabilan was saddled, but he didn't throw his leg over the pony's back. That was forbidden until Thanksgiving.

Every afternoon he put the red saddle on the pony and cinched it tight. The pony was learning already to fill his stomach out unnaturally large while the cinching was going on, and then to let it down when the straps were fixed. Sometimes Jody led him up to the brush line and let him drink from the round green tub, and sometimes he led him up through the stubble field to the hilltop from which it was possible to see the white town of Salinas and the geometric fields of the great valley, and the oak trees clipped by the sheep. Now and then they broke through the brush and came to little cleared circles so hedged in that the world was gone and only the sky and the circle of brush were left from the old life. Gabilan liked these trips and showed it by keeping his head very high and by quivering his nostrils with interest. When the two came back from an expedition they smelled of the sweet sage they had forced through.

Time dragged on toward Thanksgiving, but winter came fast. The clouds swept down and hung all day over the land and brushed the hilltops, and the winds blew shrilly at night. All day the dry oak leaves drifted down from the trees until they covered the ground, and yet the trees were unchanged.

Jody had wished it might not rain before Thanksgiving, but it did. The brown earth turned dark and the trees glistened. The cut ends of the stubble turned black with mildew; the haystacks grayed from exposure to the damp, and on the roofs the moss, which had been all summer as gray as lizards, turned a brilliant yellow-green. During the week of rain, Jody kept the pony in the box stall out of the dampness, except for a little time after school when he took him out for exercise and to drink at the water trough in the upper corral. Not once did Gabilan get wet.

The wet weather continued until little new grass appeared. Jody walked to school dressed in a slicker and short rubber boots. At length one morning the sun came out brightly. Jody, at his work in the box stall, said to Billy Buck, "Maybe I'll leave Gabilan in the corral when I go to school today."

"Be good for him to be out in the sun," Billy assured him. "No animal likes to be cooped up too long. Your father and me are going back on the hill to clean the leaves out of the spring." Billy nodded and picked his teeth with one of his little straws.

"If the rain comes, though—" Jody suggested.

"Not likely to rain today. She's rained herself out." Billy pulled up his sleeves and snapped his arm bands. "If it comes on to rain—why, a little rain don't hurt a horse."

"Well, if it does come on to rain, you put him in, will you, Billy? I'm scared he might get cold so I couldn't ride him when the time comes."

"Oh sure! I'll watch out for him if we get back in time. But it won't rain today."

And so Jody, when he went to school, left Gabilan standing out in the corral.

Billy Buck wasn't wrong about many things. He couldn't be. But he was wrong about the weather that day, for a little after noon the clouds pushed over the hills and the rain began to pour down. Jody heard it start on the schoolhouse roof. He considered holding up one finger for permission to go to the outhouse, and once outside, running for home to put the pony in. Punishment would be prompt both at school and at home. He gave it up and took ease from Billy's assurance that rain couldn't hurt a horse. When school was finally out, he hurried home through the dark rain. The banks at the sides of the road spouted little jets of muddy water. The rain slanted and swirled under a cold and gusty wind. Jody dog-trotted home, slopping through the gravelly mud of the road.

From the top of the ridge he could see Gabilan standing miserably in the corral. The red coat was almost black, and streaked with water. He stood head down with his rump to the rain and wind. Jody arrived running and threw open the barn door and led the wet pony in by his forelock. Then he found a gunny sack and rubbed the soaked hair and rubbed the legs and ankles. Gabilan stood patiently, but he trembled in gusts like the wind.

When he had dried the pony as well as he could, Jody went up to the house and brought hot water down to the barn and soaked the grain in it. Gabilan was not very hungry. He nibbled at the hot mash but he was not very much interested in it, and he still shivered now and then. A little steam rose from his damp back.

It was almost dark when Billy Buck and Carl Tiflin came home. "When the rain started we put up at Ben Herche's place, and the rain never let up all afternoon," Carl Tiflin explained. Jody looked reproachfully at Billy Buck and Billy felt guilty.

"You said it wouldn't rain," Jody accused him.

Billy looked away. "It's hard to tell, this time of year," he said, but his excuse was lame. He had no right to be fallible, and he knew it.

"The pony got wet, got soaked through."

"Did you dry him off?"

"I rubbed him with a sack and I gave him hot grain."

Billy nodded in agreement.

"Do you think he'll take cold, Billy?"

"A little rain never hurt anything," Billy assured him.

Jody's father joined the conversation then and lectured

the boy a little. "A horse," he said, "isn't any lapdog kind of thing." Carl Tiflin hated weakness and sickness, and he held a violent contempt for helplessness.

Jody's mother put a platter of steaks on the table, and boiled potatoes and boiled squash, which clouded the room with their steam. They sat down to eat. Carl Tiflin still grumbled about weakness put into animals and men by too much coddling.

Billy Buck felt bad about his mistake. "Did you blanket him?" he asked.

"No. I couldn't find any blanket. I laid some sacks over his back."

"We'll go down and cover him up after we eat, then." Billy felt better about it then. When Jody's father had gone in to the fire and his mother was washing dishes, Billy found and lighted a lantern. He and Jody walked through the mud to the barn. The barn was dark and warm and sweet. The horses still munched their evening hay. "You hold the lantern!" Billy ordered. And he felt the pony's legs and tested the heat of the flanks. He put his cheek against the pony's gray muzzle and then he rolled up the eyelids to look at the eyeballs and he lifted the lips to see the gums, and he put his fingers inside the ears. "He don't seem so chipper," Billy said. "I'll give him a rubdown."

Then Billy found a sack and rubbed the pony's legs violently and he rubbed the chest and the withers. Gabilan was strangely spiritless. He submitted patiently to the rubbing. At last Billy brought an old cotton comforter from the saddle room and threw it over the pony's back and tied it at neck and chest with string.

"Now he'll be all right in the morning," Billy said.

Jody's mother looked up when he got back to the house. "You're late up from bed," she said. She held his chin in her hard hand and brushed the tangled hair out of his eyes and she said, "Don't worry about the pony. He'll be all right. Billy's as good as any horse doctor in the country."

John Steinbeck

Jody hadn't known she could see his worry. He pulled gently away from her and knelt down in front of the fireplace until it burned his stomach. He scorched himself through and then went in to bed, but it was a hard thing to go to sleep. He awakened after what seemed a long time. The room was dark but there was a grayness in the window like that which precedes the dawn. He got up and found his overalls and searched for the legs, and then the clock in the other room struck two. He laid his clothes down and got back into bed. It was broad daylight when he awakened again. For the first time he had slept through the ringing of the triangle. He leaped up, flung on his clothes and went out of the door still buttoning his shirt. His mother looked after him for a moment and then went quietly back to her work. Her eyes were brooding and kind. Now and then her mouth smiled a little, but without changing her eyes at all.

Jody ran on toward the barn. Halfway there he heard the sound he dreaded, the hollow rasping cough of a horse. He broke into a sprint then. In the barn he found Billy Buck with the pony. Billy was rubbing its legs with his strong thick hands. He looked up and smiled gaily. "He just took a little cold," Billy said. "We'll have him out of it in a couple of days."

Jody looked at the pony's face. The eyes were half closed and the lids thick and dry. In the eye corners a crust of hard mucus stuck. Gabilan's ears hung loosely sideways and his head was low. Jody put out his hand, but the pony did not move close to it. He coughed again and his whole body constricted with the effort. A little stream of thin fluid ran from his nostrils.

Jody looked back at Billy Buck. "He's awful sick, Billy."

"Just a little cold, like I said," Billy insisted. "You go get some breakfast and then go back to school. I'll take care of him."

"But you might have to do something else. You might leave him."

106

The Gift

"No, I won't. I won't leave him at all. Tomorrow's Saturday. Then you can stay with him all day." Billy had failed again, and he felt badly about it. He had to cure the pony now.

Jody walked up to the house and took his place listlessly at the table. The eggs and bacon were cold and greasy, but he didn't notice it. He ate his usual amount. He didn't even ask to stay home from school. His mother pushed his hair back when she took his plate. "Billy'll take care of the pony," she assured him.

He moped through the whole day at school. He couldn't answer any questions nor read any words. He couldn't even tell anyone the pony was sick, for that might make him sicker. And when school was finally out he started home in dread. He walked slowly and let the other boys leave him. He wished he might continue walking and never arrive at the ranch.

Billy was in the barn, as he had promised, and the pony was worse. His eyes were almost closed now, and his breath whistled shrilly past an obstruction in his nose. A film covered that part of the eyes that was visible at all. It was doubtful whether the pony could see anymore. Now and then he snorted, to clear his nose, and by the action seemed to plug it tighter. Jody looked dispiritedly at the pony's coat. The hair lay rough and unkempt and seemed to have lost all its old luster. Billy stood quietly beside the stall. Jody hated to ask, but he had to know.

"Billy, is he—is he going to get well?"

Billy put his fingers between the bars under the pony's jaw and felt about. "Feel here," he said and he guided Jody's fingers to a large lump under the jaw. "When that gets bigger, I'll open it up and then he'll get better."

Jody looked quickly away, for he had heard about that lump. "What is it the matter with him?"

Billy didn't want to answer, but he had to. He couldn't be wrong three times. "Strangles," he said shortly, "but don't you worry about that. I'll put him out of it. I've seen them get well when they were worse than Gabilan is. I'm going to steam him now. You can help.''

"Yes," Jody said miserably. He followed Billy into the grain room and watched him make the steaming bag ready. It was a long canvas nose bag with straps to go over a horse's ears. Billy filled it one-third full of bran and then he added a couple of handfuls of dried hops. On top of the dry substance he poured a little carbolic acid and a little turpentine. "I'll be mixing it all up while you run to the house for a kettle of boiling water," Billy said.

When Jody came back with the steaming kettle, Billy buckled the straps over Gabilan's head and fitted the bag tightly around his nose. Then through a little hole in the side of the bag he poured the boiling water on the mixture. The pony started away as a cloud of strong steam rose up, but then the soothing fumes crept through his nose and into his lungs, and the sharp steam began to clear out the nasal passages. He breathed loudly. His legs trembled in an ague, and his eyes closed against the biting cloud. Billy poured in more water and kept the steam rising for fifteen minutes. At last he set down the kettle and took the bag from Gabilan's nose. The pony looked better. He breathed freely, and his eyes were open wider than they had been.

"See how good it makes him feel," Billy said. "Now we'll wrap him up in the blanket again. Maybe he'll be nearly well by morning."

"I'll stay with him tonight," Jody suggested.

"No. Don't you do it. I'll bring my blankets down here and put them in the hay. You can stay tomorrow and steam him if he needs it."

The evening was falling when they went to the house for their supper. Jody didn't even realize that someone else had fed the chickens and filled the woodbox. He walked up past the house to the dark brush line and took a drink of water from the tub. The spring water was so cold that it stung his mouth and drove a shiver through him. The sky above the hills was still light. He saw a hawk flying so high that it caught the sun on its breast and shone like a spark. Two blackbirds were driving him down the sky, glittering as they attacked their enemy. In the west, the clouds were moving in to rain again.

Jody's father didn't speak at all while the family ate supper, but after Billy Buck had taken his blankets and gone to sleep in the barn, Carl Tiflin built a high fire in the fireplace and told stories. He told about the wild man who ran naked through the country and had a tail and ears like a horse, and he told about the rabbit-cats of Moro Cojo that hopped into the trees for birds. He revived the famous Maxwell brothers who found a vein of gold and hid the traces of it so carefully that they could never find it again.

Jody sat with his chin in his hands; his mouth worked nervously, and his father gradually became aware that he wasn't listening very carefully. "Isn't that funny?" he asked.

Jody laughed politely and said, "Yes, sir." His father was angry and hurt, then. He didn't tell any more stories. After a while, Jody took a lantern and went down to the barn. Billy Buck was asleep in the hay, and except that his breath rasped a little in his lungs, the pony seemed to be much better. Jody stayed a little while, running his fingers over the red rough coat, and then he took up the lantern and went back to the house. When he was in bed, his mother came into the room.

"Have you enough covers on? It's getting winter."

"Yes, ma'am."

"Well, get some rest tonight." She hesitated to go out, stood uncertainly. "The pony will be all right," she said.

Jody was tired. He went to sleep quickly and didn't awaken until dawn. The triangle sounded, and Billy Buck came up from the barn before Jody could get out of the house.

"How is he?" Jody demanded.

Billy always wolfed his breakfast. "Pretty good. I'm going to open that lump this morning. Then he'll be better maybe."

After breakfast, Billy got out his best knife, one with a needle point. He whetted the shining blade a long time on a little carborundum stone. He tried the point and the blade again and again on his callused thumb-ball, and at last he tried it on his upper lip.

On the way to the barn, Jody noticed how the young grass was up and how the stubble was melting day by day into the new green crop of volunteer. It was a cold sunny morning.

As soon as he saw the pony, Jody knew he was worse. His eyes were closed and sealed shut with mucus. His head hung so low that his nose almost touched the straw of his bed. There was a little groan in each breath, a deep-seated, patient groan.

Billy lifted the weak head and made a quick slash with the knife. Jody saw yellow pus run out. He held up the head while Billy swabbed out the wound with weak carbolic acid salve.

"Now he'll feel better," Billy assured him. "That yellow poison is what makes him sick."

Jody looked unbelieving at Billy Buck. "He's awful sick."

Billy thought a long time what to say. He nearly tossed off a careless assurance, but he saved himself in time. "Yes, he's pretty sick," he said at last. "I've seen worse ones get well. If he doesn't get pneumonia, we'll pull him through. You stay with him. If he gets worse, you can come and get me."

For a long time after Billy went away, Jody stood beside the pony, stroking him behind the ears. The pony didn't flip his head the way he had done when he was well. The groaning in his breathing was becoming more hollow.

Doubletree Mutt looked into the barn, his big tail waving

110

provocatively, and Jody was so incensed at his health that he found a hard black clod on the floor and deliberately threw it. Doubletree Mutt went yelping away to nurse a bruised paw.

In the middle of the morning, Billy Buck came back and made another steam bag. Jody watched to see whether the pony improved this time as he had before. His breathing eased a little, but he did not raise his head.

The Saturday dragged on. Late in the afternoon Jody went to the house and brought his bedding down and made up a place to sleep in the hay. He didn't ask permission. He knew from the way his mother looked at him that she would let him do almost anything. That night he left a lantern burning on a wire over the box stall. Billy had told him to rub the pony's legs every little while.

At nine o'clock the wind sprang up and howled around the barn. And in spite of his worry, Jody grew sleepy. He got into his blankets and went to sleep, but the breathy groans of the pony sounded in his dreams. And in his sleep he heard a crashing noise which went on and on until it awakened him. The wind was rushing through the barn. He sprang up and looked down the lane of stalls. The barn door had blown open, and the pony was gone.

He caught the lantern and ran outside into the gale, and he saw Gabilan weakly shambling away into the darkness, head down, legs working slowly and mechanically. When Jody ran up and caught him by the forelock, he allowed himself to be led back and put into his stall. His groans were louder, and a fierce whistling came from his nose. Jody didn't sleep anymore then. The hissing of the pony's breath grew louder and sharper.

He was glad when Billy Buck came in at dawn. Billy looked for a time at the pony as though he had never seen him before. He felt the ears and flanks. "Jody," he said, "I've got to do something you won't want to see. You run up to the house for a while."

Jody grabbed him fiercely by the forearm. "You're not going to shoot him?"

Billy patted his hand. "No, I'm going to open a little hole in his windpipe so he can breathe. His nose is filled up. When he gets well, we'll put a little brass button in the hole for him to breathe through."

Jody couldn't have gone away if he had wanted to. It was awful to see the red hide cut, but infinitely more terrible to know it was being cut and not to see it. "I'll stay right here," he said bitterly. "You sure you got to?"

"Yes. I'm sure. If you stay, you can hold his head. If it doesn't make you sick, that is."

The fine knife came out again and was whetted again just as carefully as it had been the first time. Jody held the pony's head up and the throat taut, while Billy felt up and down for the right place. Jody sobbed once as the bright knife point disappeared into the throat. The pony plunged weakly away and then stood still, trembling violently. The blood ran thickly out and up the knife and across Billy's hand and into his shirtsleeve. The sure square hand sawed out a round hole in the flesh, and the breath came bursting out of the hole, throwing a fine spray of blood. With the rush of oxygen, the pony took a sudden strength. He lashed out with his hind feet and tried to rear, but Jody held his head down while Billy mopped the new wound with carbolic salve. It was a good job. The blood stopped flowing and the air puffed out the hole and sucked it in regularly with a little bubbling noise.

The rain brought in by the night wind began to fall on the barn roof. Then the triangle rang for breakfast. "You go up and eat while I wait," Billy said. "We've got to keep this hole from plugging up."

Jody walked slowly out of the barn. He was too dispirited to tell Billy how the barn door had blown open and let the pony out. He emerged into the wet gray morning and sloshed up to the house, taking a perverse pleasure in splashing through all the puddles. His mother fed him and put dry clothes on. She didn't question him. She seemed to know he couldn't answer questions. But when he was ready to go back to the barn she brought him a pan of steaming meal. "Give him this," she said.

But Jody did not take the pan. He said, "He won't eat anything," and ran out of the house. At the barn, Billy showed him how to fix a ball of cotton on a stick, with which to swab out the breathing hole when it became clogged with mucus.

Jody's father walked into the barn and stood with them in front of the stall. At length he turned to the boy. "Hadn't you better come with me? I'm going to drive over the hill." Jody shook his head. "You better come on, out of this," his father insisted.

Billy turned on him angrily. "Let him alone. It's his pony, isn't it?"

Carl Tiflin walked away without saying another word. His feelings were badly hurt.

All morning Jody kept the wound open and the air passing in and out freely. At noon the pony lay wearily down on his side and stretched his nose out.

Billy came back. "If you're going to stay with him tonight, you better take a little nap," he said. Jody went absently out of the barn. The sky had cleared to a hard thin blue. Everywhere the birds were busy with worms that had come to the damp surface of the ground.

Jody walked to the brush line and sat on the edge of the mossy tub. He looked down at the house and at the old bunkhouse and at the dark cypress tree. The place was familiar, but curiously changed. It wasn't itself anymore, but a frame for things that were happening. A cold wind blew out of the east now, signifying that the rain was over for a little while. At his feet Jody could see the little arms of new weeds spreading out over the ground. In the mud about the spring were thousands of quail tracks.

John Steinbeck

Doubletree Mutt came sideways and embarrassed up through the vegetable patch, and Jody, remembering how he had thrown the clod, put his arm about the dog's neck and kissed him on his wide black nose. Doubletree Mutt sat still, as though he knew some solemn thing was happening. His big tail slapped the ground gravely. Jody pulled a swollen tick out of Mutt's neck and popped it dead between his thumbnails. It was a nasty thing. He washed his hands in the cold spring water.

Except for the steady swish of the wind, the farm was very quiet. Jody knew his mother wouldn't mind if he didn't go in to eat his lunch. After a little while he went slowly back to the barn. Mutt crept into his own little house and whined softly to himself for a long time.

Billy Buck stood up from the box and surrendered the cotton swab. The pony still lay on his side and the wound in his throat bellowsed in and out. When Jody saw how dry and dead the hair looked, he knew at last that there was no hope for the pony. He had seen the dead hair before on dogs and on cows, and it was a sure sign. He sat heavily on the box and let down the barrier of the box stall. For a long time he kept his eyes on the moving wound, and at last he dozed, and the afternoon passed quickly. Just before dark his mother brought in a deep dish of stew and left it for him and went away. Jody ate a little of it, and when it was dark he set the lantern on the floor by the pony's head so he could watch the wound and keep it open. And he dozed again until the night chill awakened him. The wind was blowing fiercely, bringing the north cold with it. Jody brought a blanket from his bed in the hay and wrapped himself in it. Gabilan's breathing was quiet at last; the hole in his throat moved gently. The owls flew through the hayloft, shrieking and looking for mice. Jody put his hands down on his head and slept. In his sleep he was aware that the wind had increased. He heard it slamming about the barn.

It was daylight when he awakened. The barn door had swung open. The pony was gone. He sprang up and ran out into the morning light.

The pony's tracks were plain enough, dragging through the frostlike dew on the young grass, tired tracks with little lines between them where the hoofs had dragged. They headed for the brush line halfway up the ridge. Jody broke into a run and followed them. The sun shone on the sharp white quartz that stuck through the ground here and there. As he followed the plain trail, a shadow cut across in front of him. He looked up and saw a high circle of black buzzards, and the slowly revolving circle dropped lower and lower. The solemn birds soon disappeared over the ridge. Jody ran faster then, forced on by panic and rage. The trail entered the brush at last and followed a winding route among the tall sage bushes.

At the top of the ridge Jody was winded. He paused, puffing noisily. The blood pounded in his ears. Then he saw what he was looking for. Below, in one of the little clearings in the brush, lay the red pony. In the distance, Jody could see the legs moving slowly and convulsively. And in a circle around him stood the buzzards, waiting for the moment of death they know so well.

Jody leaped forward and plunged down the hill. The wet ground muffled his steps and the brush hid him. When he arrived, it was all over. The first buzzard sat on the pony's head and its beak had just risen dripping with dark eye fluid. Jody plunged into the circle like a cat. The black brotherhood arose in a cloud, but the big one on the pony's head was too late. As it hopped along to take off, Jody caught its wing tip and pulled it down. It was nearly as big as he was. The free wing crashed into his face with the force of a club, but he hung on. The claws fastened on his leg and the wing elbows battered his head on either side. Jody groped blindly with his free hand. His fingers found the neck of the struggling bird. The red eyes looked into his face, calm and fearless and fierce; the naked head turned from side to side. Then the beak opened and vomited a stream of putrefied fluid. Jody brought up his knee and fell on the great bird. He held the neck to the ground with one hand while his other found a piece of sharp white quartz. The first blow broke the beak sideways and black blood spurted from the twisted, leathery mouth corners. He struck again and missed. The red fearless eyes still looked at him, impersonal and unafraid and detached. He struck again and again, until the buzzard lay dead, until its head was a red pulp. He was still beating the dead bird when Billy Buck pulled him off and held him tightly to calm his shaking.

Carl Tiflin wiped the blood from the boy's face with a red bandana. Jody was limp and quiet now. His father moved the buzzard with his toe. "Jody," he explained, "the buzzard didn't kill the pony. Don't you know that?"

"I know it," Jody said wearily.

It was Billy Buck who was angry. He had lifted Jody in his arms and had turned to carry him home. But he turned back on Carl Tiflin. "'Course he knows it!" Billy said furiously. "Can't you see how he'd feel about it?"

METZENGERSTEIN

EDGAR ALLAN POE

Horror and fatality have been stalking abroad in all ages. Why then give a date to the story I have to tell? Let it suffice to say, that at the period of which I speak, there existed, in the interior of Hungary, a settled although hidden belief in the doctrines of the Metempsychosis. Of the doctrines themselves—that is, of their falsity, or of their probability—I say nothing.

The families of Berlifitzing and Metzengerstein had been at variance for centuries. Never before were two houses so illustrious, mutually embittered by hostility so deadly. The origin of this enmity seems to be found in the words of an ancient prophecy—"A lofty name shall have a fearful fall when, as the rider over his horse, the mortality of Metzengerstein shall triumph over the immortality of Berlifitzing."

To be sure, the words themselves had little or no meaning. But more trivial causes have given rise—and that no long while ago—to consequences equally eventful. Besides, the estates, which were contiguous, had long exercised a rival influence in the affairs of a busy government. Moreover, near neighbors are seldom friends; and the inhabitants of the Castle Berlifitzing might look, from their lofty buttresses, into the very windows of the Palace Metzengerstein. Least of all had the more than feudal magnificence, thus discovered, a tendency to allay the irritable feelings of the less ancient and less wealthy Berlifitzings. What wonder, then, that the words, however silly, of that prediction, should have succeeded in setting and keeping at variance two families already predisposed to quarrel by every instigation of hereditary jealousy? The prophecy seemed to imply—if it implied anything—a final triumph on the part of the already more powerful house; and was of course remembered with the more bitter animosity by the weaker and less influential.

Wilhelm, Count Berlifitzing, although loftily descended, was, at the epoch of this narrative, an infirm and doting old man, remarkable for nothing but an inordinate and inveterate personal antipathy to the family of his rival, and so passionate a love of horses, and of hunting, that neither bodily infirmity, great age, nor mental incapacity, prevented his daily participation in the dangers of the chase.

Frederick, Baron Metzengerstein, was, on the other hand, not yet of age. His father, the Minister G——, died young. His mother, the Lady Mary, followed him quickly. Frederick was, at that time, in his eighteenth year. In a city, eighteen years are no long period; but in a wilderness—in so magnificent a wilderness as that old principality, the pendulum vibrates with a deeper meaning.

From some peculiar circumstances attending the administration of his father, the young Baron, at the decease of the former, entered immediately upon his vast possessions. Such estates were seldom held before by a nobleman of Hungary. His castles were without number. The chief in point of splendor and extent was the "Palace Metzengerstein." The boundary line of his dominions was never clearly defined; but his principal park embraced a circuit of fifty miles.

Upon the succession of a proprietor so young, with a character so well known, to a fortune so unparalleled, little speculation was afloat in regard to his probable course of conduct. And, indeed, for the space of three days, the behavior of the heir out-Heroded Herod, and fairly surpassed the expectations of his most enthusiastic admirers. Shameful debaucheries—flagrant treacheries—unheard-of atrocities—gave his trembling vassals quickly to understand that no servile submission on their part—no punctilios of conscience on his own—were thenceforward to prove any security against the remorseless fangs of a petty Caligula. On the night of the fourth day, the stables of the Castle Berlifitzing were discovered to be on fire; and the unanimous opinion of the neighborhood added the crime of the incendiary to the already hideous list of the Baron's misdemeanors and enormities.

But during the tumult occasioned by this occurrence, the young nobleman himself sat apparently buried in meditation, in a vast and desolate upper apartment of the family palace of Metzengerstein. The rich although faded tapestry hangings which swung gloomily upon the walls, represented the shadowy and majestic forms of a thousand illustrious ancestors. *Here,* rich-ermined priests, and pontifical dignitaries, familiarly seated with the autocrat and the sovereign, put a veto on the wishes of a temporal king, or restrained with the fiat of papal supremacy the rebellious sceptre of the Arch-enemy. *There,* the dark, tall statures of the Princes Metzengerstein—their muscular war-coursers plunging over the carcasses of fallen foes—startled the steadiest nerves with their vigorous expression; and *here,* again, the voluptuous and swan-like figures of the dames of days gone by, floated away in the mazes of an unreal dance to the strains of imaginary melody.

But as the Baron listened, or affected to listen, to the gradually increasing uproar in the stables of Berlifitzing— or perhaps pondered upon some more novel, some more decided act of audacity—his eyes were turned unwittingly to the figure of an enormous, and unnaturally colored

121

horse, represented in the tapestry as belonging to a Saracen ancestor of the family of his rival. The horse itself, in the foreground of the design, stood motionless and statue-like—while, farther back, its discomfited rider perished by the dagger of a Metzengerstein.

On Frederick's lips arose a fiendish expression, as he became aware of the direction which his glance had, without his consciousness, assumed. Yet he did not remove it. On the contrary, he could by no means account for the overwhelming anxiety which appeared falling like a pall upon his senses. It was with difficulty that he reconciled his dreamy and incoherent feelings with the certainty of being awake. The longer he gazed the more absorbing became the spell—the more impossible did it appear that he could ever withdraw his glance from the fascination of that tapestry. But the tumult without becoming suddenly more violent, with a compulsory exertion he diverted his attention to the glare of ruddy light thrown full by the flaming stables upon the windows of the apartment.

The action, however, was but momentary; his gaze returned mechanically to the wall. To his extreme horror and astonishment, the head of the gigantic steed had, in the meantime, altered its position. The neck of the animal, before arched, as if in compassion, over the prostrate body of its lord, was now extended, at full length, in the direction of the Baron. The eyes, before invisible, now wore an energetic and human expression, while they gleamed with a fiery and unusual red; and the distended lips of the apparently enraged horse left in full view his sepulchral and disgusting teeth.

Stupefied with terror, the young nobleman tottered to the door. As he threw it open, a flash of red light, streaming far into the chamber, flung his shadow with a clear outline against the quivering tapestry; and he shuddered to perceive that shadow—as he staggered awhile upon the threshold—assuming the exact position, and precisely fill-

ing up the contour, of the relentless and triumphant murderer of the Saracen Berlifitzing.

To lighten the depression of his spirits, the Baron hurried into the open air. At the principal gate of the palace he encountered three equerries. With much difficulty, and at the imminent peril of their lives, they were restraining the convulsive plunges of a gigantic and fiery-colored horse.

"Whose horse? Where did you get him?" demanded the youth, in a querulous and husky tone, as he became instantly aware that the mysterious steed in the tapestried chamber was the very counterpart of the furious animal before his eyes.

"He is your own property, sire," replied one of the equerries, "at least he is claimed by no other owner. We caught him flying, all smoking and foaming with rage, from the burning stables of the Castle Berlifitzing. Supposing him to have belonged to the Old Count's stud of foreign horses, we led him back as an estray. But the grooms there disclaim any title to the creature; which is strange, since he bears evident marks of having made a narrow escape from the flames."

"The letters W. V. B. are also branded very distinctly on his forehead," interrupted a second equerry: "I supposed them, of course, to be the initials of William Von Berlifitzing—but all at the castle are positive in denying any knowledge of the horse."

"Extremely singular!" said the young Baron, with a musing air, and apparently unconscious of the meaning of his words. "He is, as you say, a remarkable horse—a prodigious horse! although, as you very justly observe, of a suspicious and untractable character; let him be mine, however," he added, after a pause, "perhaps a rider like Frederick of Metzengerstein may tame even the devil from the stables of Berlifitzing."

"You are mistaken, my lord; the horse, as I think we mentioned, is *not* from the stables of the Count. If such had been the case, we know our duty better than to bring him into the presence of a noble of your family."

"True!" observed the Baron, drily; and at that instant a page of the bed-chamber came from the palace with a heightened color, and a precipitate step. He whispered into his master's ear an account of the sudden disappearance of a small portion of the tapestry, in an apartment which he designated; entering, at the same time, into particulars of a minute and circumstantial character; but from the low tone of voice in which these latter were communicated, nothing escaped to gratify the excited curiosity of the equerries.

The young Frederick, during the conference, seemed agitated by a variety of emotions. He soon, however, recovered his composure, and an expression of determined malignancy settled upon his countenance, as he gave peremptory orders that the apartment in question should be immediately locked up, and the key placed in his own possession.

"Have you heard of the unhappy death of the old hunter Berlifitzing?" said one of his vassals to the Baron, as, after the departure of the page, the huge steed which that nobleman had adopted as his own, plunged and curveted, with redoubled fury, down the long avenue which extended from the palace to the stables of Metzengerstein.

"No!" said the Baron, turning abruptly toward the speaker. "Dead! say you?"

"It is indeed true, my lord; and, to the noble of your name, will be, I imagine, no unwelcome intelligence."

A rapid smile shot over the countenance of the listener. "How died he?"

"In his rash exertions to rescue a favorite portion of the hunting stud, he has himself perished miserably in the flames."

"I–n–d–e–e–d!" ejaculated the Baron, as if slowly and deliberately impressed with the truth of some exciting idea.

"Indeed," repeated the vassal.

"Shocking!" said the youth, calmly, and turned quietly into the palace.

From this date a marked alteration took place in the outward demeanor of the dissolute young Baron Frederick Von Metzengerstein. Indeed, his behavior disappointed every expectation, and proved little in accordance with the views of many a maneuvering mamma; while his habits and manner, still less than formerly, offered anything congenial with those of the neighboring aristocracy. He was never to be seen beyond the limits of his own domain, and, in his wide and social world, was utterly companionless—unless, indeed, that unnatural, impetuous, and fiery-colored horse, which he henceforward continually bestrode, had any mysterious right to the title of his friend.

Numerous invitations on the part of the neighborhood for a long time, however, periodically came in. "Will the Baron honor our festivals with his presence?" "Will the Baron join us in a hunting of the boar?"—"Metzengerstein does not hunt"; "Metzengerstein will not attend," were the haughty and laconic answers.

These repeated insults were not to be endured by an imperious nobility. Such invitations became less cordial—less frequent—in time they ceased altogether. The widow of the unfortunate Count Berlifitzing was even heard to express a hope "that the Baron might be at home when he did not wish to be at home, since he disdained the company of his equals; and ride when he did not wish to ride, since he preferred the society of a horse." This to be sure was a very silly explosion of hereditary pique; and merely proved how singularly unmeaning our sayings are apt to become, when we desire to be unusually energetic.

The charitable, nevertheless, attributed the alteration in the conduct of the young nobleman to the natural sorrow of a son for the untimely loss of his parents;—forgetting, however, his atrocious and reckless behavior during the short period immediately succeeding that bereavement. Some there were, indeed, who suggested a too haughty idea of self-consequence and dignity. Others again (among whom may be mentioned the family physician) did not hesitate in speaking of morbid melancholy, and hereditary ill-health; while dark hints, of a more equivocal nature, were current among the multitude.

Indeed, the Baron's perverse attachment to his lately-acquired charger—an attachment which seemed to attain new strength from every fresh example of the animal's ferocious and demon-like propensities—at length became, in the eyes of all reasonable men, a hideous and unnatural fervor. In the glare of noon—at the dead hour of night—in sickness or in health—in calm or in tempest—the young Metzengerstein seemed riveted to the saddle of that colossal horse, whose intractable audacities so well accorded with his own spirit.

There were circumstances, moreover, which, coupled with late events, gave an unearthly and portentous character to the mania of the rider, and to the capabilities of the steed. The space passed over in a single leap had been accurately measured, and was found to exceed, by an astounding difference, the wildest expectations of the most imaginative. The Baron, besides, had no particular *name* for the animal, although all the rest in his collection were distinguished by characteristic appellations. His stable, too, was appointed at a distance from the rest; and with regard to grooming and other necessary offices, none but the owner in person had ventured to officiate, or even to enter the enclosure of that horse's particular stall. It was also to be observed, that although the three grooms, who had caught the steed as he fled from the conflagration at Berlifitzing, had succeeded in arresting his course, by means of a chain-bridle and noose—yet not one of the three could with any certainty affirm that he had, during that dangerous struggle, or at any period thereafter, actually placed his hand upon the body of the beast. Instances of peculiar intelligence in the demeanor of a noble and high-spirited horse are not to be supposed capable of exciting unreasonable attention, but there were certain circumstances which intruded themselves by force upon the most skeptical and phlegmatic; and it is said there were times when the animal caused the gaping crowd who stood around to recoil in horror from the deep and impressive meaning of his terrible stamp—times when the young Metzengerstein turned pale and shrunk away from the rapid and searching expression of his human-looking eye.

Among all the retinue of the Baron, however, none were found to doubt the ardor of that extraordinary affection which existed on the part of the young nobleman for the fiery qualities of his horse; at least, none but an insignificant and misshapen little page, whose deformities were in everybody's way, and whose opinions were of the least possible importance. He (if his ideas are worth mentioning at all) had the effrontery to assert that his master never vaulted into the saddle without an unaccountable and almost imperceptible shudder; and that, upon his return from every long-continued and habitual ride, an expression of triumphant malignity distorted every muscle in his countenance.

One tempestuous night, Metzengerstein, awaking from a heavy slumber, descended like a maniac from his chamber, and, mounting in hot haste, bounded away into the mazes of the forest. An occurrence so common attracted no particular attention, but his return was looked for with intense anxiety on the part of his domestics, when, after some hours' absence, the stupendous and magnificent battlements of the Palace Metzengerstein, were discovered crackling and rocking to their very foundation, under the influence of a dense and livid mass of ungovernable fire.

As the flames, when first seen, had already made so terrible a progress that all efforts to save any portion of the building were evidently futile, the astonished neighborhood stood idly around in silent if not pathetic wonder. But a new and fearful object soon riveted the attention of the multitude, and proved how much more intense is the excitement wrought in the feelings of a crowd by the contemplation of human agony, than that brought about by the most appalling spectacles of inanimate matter.

Up the long avenue of aged oaks which led from the forest to the main entrance of the Palace Metzengerstein, a steed, bearing an unbonneted and disordered rider, was seen leaping with an impetuosity which outstripped the very Demon of the Tempest.

The career of the horseman was indisputably, on his own part, uncontrollable. The agony of his countenance, the convulsive struggle of his frame, gave evidence of superhuman exertion: but no sound, save a solitary shriek, escaped from his lacerated lips, which were bitten through and through in the intensity of terror. One instant, and the clattering of hoofs resounded sharply and shrilly above the roaring of the flames and the shrieking of the winds—another, and, clearing at a single plunge the gateway and the moat, the steed bounded far up the tottering staircases of the palace, and, with its rider, disappeared amid the whirlwind of chaotic fire.

The fury of the tempest immediately died away, and a dead calm sullenly succeeded. A white flame still enveloped the building like a shroud, and, streaming far away into the quiet atmosphere, shot forth a glare of preternatural light; while a cloud of smoke settled heavily over the battlements in the distinct colossal figure of—*a horse*.

THE STORY OF THE ENCHANTED HORSE

(from *Tales from the Arabian Nights*)

On the festival of the Nooroze, which is the first day of the year and of spring, the Sultan of Shiraz was just concluding his public audience, when a Hindu appeared at the foot of the throne with an artificial horse, so spiritedly modeled that at first sight he was taken for a living animal.

The Hindu prostrated himself before the throne, and pointing to the horse, said to the Sultan, "This horse is a great wonder; if I wish to be transported to the most distant parts of the earth, I have only to mount him. I offer to show your Majesty this wonder if you command me."

The Sultan, who was very fond of everything that was curious, and who had never beheld or heard anything quite so strange as this, told the Hindu that he would like to see him perform what he had promised.

The Hindu at once put his foot into the stirrup, swung himself into the saddle, and asked the Sultan whither he wished him to go.

"Do you see yonder mountain?" said the Sultan, pointing to it. "Ride your horse there, and bring me a branch from the palm tree that grows at the foot of the hill."

No sooner had the Sultan spoken than the Hindu turned a peg, which was in the hollow of the horse's neck, just by the pommel of the saddle. Instantly the horse rose from the ground, and bore his rider into the air with the speed of lightning, to the amazement of the Sultan and all the spectators. Within less than a quarter of an hour they saw him returning with the palm branch in his hand. Alighting amidst the acclamations of the people, he dismounted and, approaching the throne, laid the palm branch at the Sultan's feet.

The Sultan, still marveling at this unheard-of sight, was filled with a great desire to possess the horse, and said to the Hindu, "I will buy him of you, if he is for sale."

"Sire," replied the Hindu, "there is only one condition on which I will part with my horse, namely, the hand of the Princess, your daughter, as my wife."

The courtiers surrounding the Sultan's throne could not restrain their laughter at the Hindu's extravagant proposal. But Prince Feroze Shah, the Sultan's eldest son, was very indignant. "Sire," said he, "I hope that you will at once refuse this impudent demand, and not allow this miserable juggler to flatter himself for a moment with the hope of a marriage with one of the most powerful houses in the world. Think what you owe to yourself and to your noble blood!"

"My son," replied the Sultan, "I will not grant him what he asks. But putting my daughter the Princess out of the question, I may make a different bargain with him. First, however, I wish you to examine the horse; try him yourself, and tell me what you think of him."

On hearing this the Hindu eagerly ran forward to help the Prince mount, and show him how to guide and manage the horse. But without waiting for the Hindu's assistance, the Prince mounted and turned the peg as he had seen the other do. Instantly the horse darted into the air, swift as an arrow shot from a bow; and in a few moments neither horse nor Prince could be seen. The Hindu, alarmed at what had happened, threw himself before the throne and begged the Sultan not to be angry.

"Your Majesty," he said, "saw as well as I with what

speed the horse flew away. The surprise took away my power of speech. But even if I could have spoken to advise him, he was already too far away to hear me. There is still room to hope, however, that the Prince will discover that there is another peg, and as soon as he turns that, the horse will cease to rise, and will descend gently to the ground."

Notwithstanding these arguments the Sultan was much alarmed at his son's evident danger, and said to the Hindu, "Your head shall answer for my son's life, unless he returns safe in three months' time, or unless I hear that he is alive." He then ordered his officers to secure the Hindu and keep him a close prisoner; after which he retired to his palace, sorrowing that the Festival of Nooroze had ended so unluckily.

Meanwhile, the Prince was carried through the air with fearful rapidity. In less than an hour he had mounted so high that the mountains and plains below him all seemed to melt together. Then for the first time he began to think of returning, and to this end he began turning the peg, first one way and then the other, at the same time pulling upon the bridle. But when he found that the horse continued to ascend he was greatly alarmed, and deeply repented of his folly in not learning to guide the horse before he mounted. He now began to examine the horse's head and neck very carefully, and discovered behind the right ear a second peg, smaller than the first. He turned this peg and presently felt that he was descending in the same oblique manner as he had mounted, but not so swiftly.

Night was already approaching when the Prince discovered and turned the small peg; and as the horse descended he gradually lost sight of the sun's last setting rays, until presently it was quite dark. He was obliged to let the bridle hang loose, and wait patiently for the horse to choose his own landing place, whether it might be in the desert, in the river or in the sea.

The Story of the Enchanted Horse

At last, about midnight, the horse stopped upon solid ground, and the Prince dismounted, faint with hunger, for he had eaten nothing since the morning. He found himself on the terrace of a magnificent palace; and groping about, he presently reached a staircase which led down into an apartment, the door of which was half open.

The Prince stopped and listened at the door, then advanced cautiously into the room, and by the light of a lamp saw a number of black slaves, sleeping with their naked swords beside them. This was evidently the guard chamber of some Sultan or Princess. Advancing on tiptoe, he drew aside the curtain and saw a magnificent chamber, containing many beds, one of which was placed higher than the others on a raised dais—evidently the beds of the Princess and her women. He crept softly toward the dais, and beheld a beauty so extraordinary that he was charmed at the first sight. He fell on his knees and gently twitched the sleeve of the Princess, who opened her eyes and was greatly surprised to see a handsome young man bending over her, yet showed no sign of fear. The Prince rose to his feet, and, bowing to the ground, said:

"Beautiful Princess, through a most extraordinary adventure you see at your feet a suppliant Prince, son of the Sultan of Persia, who prays for your assistance and protection."

In answer to this appeal of Prince Feroze Shah, the beautiful Princess said:

"Prince, you are not in a barbarous country, but in the kingdom of the Rajah of Bengal. This is his country estate, and I am his eldest daughter. I grant you the protection that you ask, and you may depend upon my word."

The Prince of Persia would have thanked the Princess, but she would not let him speak. "Impatient though I am," said she, "to know by what miracle you have come here from the capital of Persia, and by what enchantment you escaped the watchfulness of my guards, yet I will restrain my curiosity until later, after you have rested from your fatigue.''

The Princess's women were much surprised to see a Prince in her bedchamber, but they at once prepared to obey her command, and conducted him into a handsome apartment. Here, while some prepared the bed, others brought and served a welcome and bountiful supper.

The next day the Princess prepared to receive the Prince, and took more pains in dressing and adorning herself than she ever had done before. She decked her neck, head and arms with the finest diamonds she possessed, and clothed herself in the richest fabric of the Indies, of a most beautiful color, and made only for Kings, Princes, and Princesses. After once more consulting her glass, she sent word to the Prince of Persia that she would receive him.

The Prince, who had just finished dressing when he received the Princess's message, hastened to avail himself of the honor conferred on him. He told her of the wonders of the Enchanted Horse, of his wonderful journey through the air, and of the means by which he had gained entrance to her chamber. Then, after thanking her for her kind reception, he expressed a wish to return home and relieve the anxiety of the Sultan his father. The Princess replied:

''I cannot approve, Prince, of your leaving so soon. Grant me the favor of a somewhat longer visit, so that you may take back to the court of Persia a better account of what you have seen in the Kingdom of Bengal.''

The Prince could not well refuse the Princess this favor, after the kindness she had shown him; and she busied herself with plans for hunting parties, concerts, and magnificent feasts to render his stay agreeable.

For two whole months the Prince of Persia abandoned himself entirely to the will of the Princess, who seemed to think that he had nothing to do but pass his whole life with her. But at last he declared that he could stay no longer, and begged leave to return to his father.

"And, Princess," he added, "if I were not afraid of giving offense, I would ask the favor of taking you along with me."

The Princess made no answer to this address of the Prince of Persia; but her silence and downcast eyes told him plainly that she had no reluctance to accompany him. Her only fear, she confessed, was that the Prince might not know well enough how to govern the horse. But the Prince soon removed her fear by assuring her that after the experience he had had, he defied the Hindu himself to manage the horse better. Accordingly they gave all their thoughts to planning how to get away secretly from the palace, without anyone having a suspicion of their design.

The next morning, a little before daybreak, when all the attendants were still asleep, they made their way to the terrace of the palace. The Prince turned the horse toward Persia, and as soon as the Princess had mounted behind him and was well settled with her arms about his waist, he turned the peg, whereupon the horse mounted into the air with his accustomed speed, and in two hours' time they came in sight of the Persian capital.

Instead of alighting at the palace, the Prince directed his course to a kiosk a little distance outside the city. He led the Princess into a handsome apartment, ordered the attendants to provide her with whatever she needed, and told her that he would return immediately after informing his father of their arrival. Thereupon he ordered a horse to be brought and set out for the palace.

The Sultan received his son with tears of joy, and listened eagerly while the Prince related his adventures during his flight through the air, his kind reception at the palace of the Princess of Bengal, and his long stay there due to their mutual affection. He added that, having promised to marry her, he had persuaded her to accompany him to Persia. "I brought her with me on the Enchanted Horse," he concluded, "and left her in your summer palace till I could return and assure her of your consent."

Upon hearing these words, the Sultan embraced his son a second time, and said to him, "My son, I not only consent to your marriage with the Princess of Bengal, but will myself go and bring her to the palace, and your wedding shall be celebrated this very day."

The Sultan now ordered that the Hindu should be released from prison and brought before him. When this was done, the Sultan said, "I held you prisoner that your life might answer for that of the Prince, my son. Thanks be to God, he has returned in safety. Go, take your horse, and never let me see your face again."

The Hindu had learned of those who brought him from prison, all about the Princess whom Prince Feroze Shah had brought with him and left at the kiosk, and at once he began to think of revenge. He mounted his horse and flew directly to the kiosk, where he told the Captain of the Guard that he came with orders to conduct the Princess of Bengal through the air to the Sultan, who awaited her in the great square of his palace.

The Captain of the Guard, seeing that the Hindu had been released from prison, believed his story. And the Princess at once consented to do what the Prince, as she thought, desired of her.

The Hindu, overjoyed at the ease with which his wicked plan was succeeding, mounted his horse, took the Princess up behind him, turned the peg, and instantly the horse mounted into the air.

Meanwhile, the Sultan of Persia, attended by his court, was on the road to the kiosk where the Princess of Bengal had been left, while the Prince himself had hurried on ahead to prepare the Princess to receive his father. Suddenly the Hindu, to brave them both, and avenge himself for the ill-treatment he had received, appeared over their heads with his prize.

When the Sultan saw the Hindu, his surprise and anger were all the more keen because it was out of his power to punish his outrageous act. He could only stand and hurl a thousand maledictions at him, as did also the courtiers who had witnessed this unequaled piece of insolence. But the grief of Prince Feroze Shah was indescribable when he beheld the Hindu bearing away the Princess whom he loved so passionately. He made his way, melancholy and brokenhearted, to the kiosk where he had last taken leave of the Princess. Here, the Captain of the Guard, who had already learned of the Hindu's treachery, threw himself at the Prince's feet, and condemned himself to die by his own hand, because of his fatal credulity.

"Rise," said the Prince, "I blame, not you, but my own want of precaution, for the loss of my Princess. But lose no time, bring me a dervish's robe, and take care that you give no hint that it is for me."

When the Captain of the Guard had procured the dervish's robe, the Prince at once disguised himself in it, and taking with him a box of jewels, left the palace, resolved not to return until he had found his Princess or perish in the attempt.

Meanwhile, the Hindu, mounted on his Enchanted Horse, with the Princess behind him, arrived at the capital of the Kingdom of Kashmir. He did not enter the city, but alighted in a wood, and left the Princess on a grassy spot close to a rivulet of fresh water, while he went to seek food. On his return, and after he and the Princess had partaken of refreshment, he began to maltreat the Princess, because she refused to become his wife.

Now it happened that the Sultan of Kashmir and his court were passing through the wood on their return from hunting, and hearing a woman's voice calling for help, went to her rescue. The Hindu with great impudence asked what business anyone had to interfere, since the lady was his wife! Whereupon the Princess cried out:

"My Lord, whoever you are whom Heaven has sent to my assistance, have compassion on me! I am a Princess. This Hindu is a wicked magician who has forced me away from the Prince of Persia, whom I was to marry, and has brought me hither on the Enchanted Horse that you see there."

The Princess's beauty, majestic air, and tears all declared that she spoke the truth. Justly enraged at the Hindu's insolence, the Sultan of Kashmir ordered his guards to seize him and strike off his head, which sentence was immediately carried out.

The Princess's joy was unbounded at finding herself rescued from the wicked Hindu. She supposed that the Sultan of Kashmir would at once restore her to the Prince of Persia, but she was much deceived in these hopes. For her rescuer had resolved to marry her himself the next day, and issued a proclamation commanding the general rejoicing of the inhabitants.

The Princess of Bengal was awakened at break of day by drums and trumpets and sounds of joy throughout the palace, but was far from guessing the true cause. When the Sultan came to wait upon her, he explained that these rejoicings were in honor of their marriage, and begged her to consent to the union. On hearing this the Princess fainted away.

The servingwomen who were present ran to her assistance, but it was long before they could bring her back to consciousness. When at last she recovered, she resolved that sooner than be forced to marry the Sultan of Kashmir she would pretend that she had gone mad. Accordingly she began to talk wildly, and show other signs of a disordered mind, even springing from her seat as if to attack the Sultan, so that he became greatly alarmed and sent for all the court physicians to ask if they could cure her of her disease.

When he found that his court physicians could not cure

142

her, he sent for the most famous doctors in his kingdom, who had no better success. Next, he sent word to the courts of neighboring Sultans with promises of generous reward to anyone who could cure her malady. Physicians arrived from all parts, and tried their skill, but none could boast of success.

Meanwhile, Prince Feroze Shah, disguised as a dervish, traveled through many provinces and towns, everywhere inquiring about his lost Princess. At last in a certain city of Hindustan he learned of a Princess of Bengal who had gone mad on the day of her intended marriage with the Sultan of Kashmir. Convinced that there could be but one Princess of Bengal, he hastened to the capital of Kashmir and upon arriving was told the story of the Princess, and the fate of the Hindu magician. The Prince was now convinced that he had at last found the beloved object of his long search.

Providing himself with the distinctive dress of a physician, he went boldly to the palace and announced his wish to be allowed to attempt the cure of the Princess. Since it was now some time since any physician had offered himself, the Sultan had begun to lose hope of ever seeing the Princess cured, though he still wished to marry her. So he at once ordered the new physician to be brought before him; and upon the Prince being admitted, told him that the Princess could not bear the sight of a physician without falling into the most violent paroxysms. Accordingly he conducted the Prince to a closet from which he might see her through a lattice without himself being seen. There Feroze Shah beheld his lovely Princess sitting in hopeless sorrow, the tears flowing from her beautiful eyes, while she sang a plaintive air deploring her unhappy fate. Upon leaving the closet, the Prince told the Sultan that he had assured himself that the Princess's complaint was not incurable, but that if he was to aid her he must speak with her in private and alone.

The Sultan ordered the Princess's chamber door to be opened, and Feroze Shah went in. Immediately the

Princess resorted to her old practice of meeting physicians with threats, and indications of attacking them. But Feroze Shah came close to her and said in so low a voice that only she could hear, "Princess, I am not a physician, but Feroze Shah, and have come to obtain your liberty."

The Princess, who knew the sound of his voice, and recognized him, notwithstanding he had let his beard grow so long, grew calm at once, and was filled with secret joy at the unexpected sight of the Prince she loved. After they had briefly informed each other of all that had happened since their separation, the Prince asked if she knew what had become of the horse after the death of the Hindu magician. She replied that she did not know, but supposed that he was carefully guarded as a curiosity. Feroze Shah then told the Princess that he intended to obtain and use the horse to convey them both back to Persia; and they planned together, as the first step to this end, that the Princess the next day should receive the Sultan.

On the following day the Sultan was overjoyed to find that the Princess's cure was apparently far advanced, and regarded the Prince as the greatest physician in the world. The Prince of Persia, who accompanied the Sultan on his visit to the Princess, inquired of him how she had come into the Kingdom of Kashmir from her far-distant country.

The Sultan then repeated the story of the Hindu magician, adding that the Enchanted Horse was kept safely in his treasury as a great curiosity, though he knew not how to use it.

"Sire," replied the pretended physician, "this information affords me a means of curing the Princess. When she was brought hither on the Enchanted Horse, she contracted part of the enchantment, which can be dispelled only by a certain incense of which I have knowledge. Let the horse be brought tomorrow into the great square before the palace, and leave the rest to me. I promise to show you and all your assembled people, in a few moments' time, the Princess of

144

Bengal completely restored in body and mind. But to assure the success of what I propose, the Princess must be dressed as magnificently as possible and adorned with the most valuable jewels in your treasury.''

All this the Sultan eagerly promised, for he would have undertaken far more difficult things to assure his marriage with the Princess.

The next day the Enchanted Horse was taken from the treasury and brought to the great square before the palace. The rumor of something extraordinary having spread through the town, crowds of people flocked thither from all sides. The Sultan of Kashmir, surrounded by his nobles and ministers of state, occupied a gallery erected for the purpose. The Princess of Bengal, attended by her ladies in waiting, went up to the Enchanted Horse, and the women helped her to mount. The pretended physician then placed around the horse many vessels full of burning charcoal, into which he cast handfuls of incense. After which, he ran three times about the horse, pretending to utter certain magic words. The pots sent forth a dark cloud of smoke that surrounded the Princess, so that neither she nor the horse could be seen. The Prince mounted nimbly behind her and turned the peg; and as the horse rose with them into the air, the Sultan distinctly heard these words, "Sultan of Kashmir, when you marry Princesses who implore your protection, learn first to obtain their consent!"

Thus the Prince delivered the Princess of Bengal, and carried her that same day to the capital of Persia where the Sultan his father made immediate preparation for the solemnization of their marriage with all fitting pomp and magnificence. After the days appointed for rejoicing were over, the Sultan named and appointed an ambassador to go to the Rajah of Bengal, to ask his approval of the alliance contracted by this marriage; which the Rajah of Bengal took as an honor, and granted with great pleasure and satisfaction.

BLACK BEAUTY

ANNA SEWELL

(an excerpt)

The first place that I can well remember was a large pleasant meadow with a pond of clear water in it. Some shady trees leaned over it, and rushes and water lilies grew at the deep end. Over the hedge on one side we looked into a plowed field, and on the other we looked over a gate at our master's house, which stood by the roadside; at the top of the meadow was a plantation of fir trees, and at the bottom a running brook overhung by a steep bank.

While I was young I lived upon my mother's milk, as I could not eat grass. In the daytime I ran by her side, and at night I lay down close by her. When it was hot, we used to stand by the pond in the shade of the trees, and when it was cold, we had a nice warm shed near the plantation.

As soon as I was old enough to eat grass, my mother used to go out to work in the daytime, and come back in the evening.

There were six young colts in the meadow besides me; they were older than I was; some were nearly as large as grown-up horses. I used to run with them, and had great fun; we used to gallop all together round and round the field, as hard as we could go. Sometimes we had rather rough play, for they would frequently bite and kick as well as gallop.

149

Anna Sewell

One day, when there was a good deal of kicking, my mother whinnied to me to come to her, and then she said:

"I wish you to pay attention to what I am going to say to you. The colts who live here are very good colts, but they are cart-horse colts, and, of course, they have not learned manners. You have been well bred and well born; your father has a great name in these parts, and your grandfather won the cup two years at the Newmarket races; your grandmother had the sweetest temper of any horse I ever knew, and I think you have never seen me kick or bite. I hope you will grow up gentle and good, and never learn bad ways; do your work with a good will, lift your feet up well when you trot, and never bite or kick even in play."

I have never forgotten my mother's advice; I knew she was a wise old horse, and our master thought a great deal of her. Her name was Duchess, but he often called her Pet.

Our master was a good, kind man. He gave us good food, good lodging, and kind words; he spoke as kindly to us as he did to his little children. We were all fond of him, and my mother loved him very much. When she saw him at the gate, she would neigh with joy, and trot up to him. He would pat and stroke her and say, "Well, old Pet, and how is your little Darkie?" I was a dull black, so he called me Darkie; then he would give me a piece of bread, which was very good, and sometimes he brought a carrot for my mother. All the horses would come to him, but I think we were his favorites. My mother always took him to the town on a market day in a light gig.

There was a plowboy, Dick, who sometimes came into our field to pluck blackberries from the hedge. When he had eaten all he wanted, he would have what he called fun with the colts, throwing stones and sticks at them to make them gallop. We did not much mind him, for we could gallop off; but sometimes a stone would hit and hurt us.

One day he was at this game, and did not know that the master was in the next field; but he was there, watching

150

what was going on; over the hedge he jumped in a snap, and catching Dick by the arm, he gave him such a box on the ear as made him roar with the pain and surprise. As soon as we saw the master, we trotted up nearer to see what went on.

"Bad boy!" he said, "bad boy! to chase the colts. This is not the first time, nor the second, but it shall be the last. There—take your money and go home. I shall not want you on my farm again." So we never saw Dick any more. Old Daniel, the man who looked after the horses, was just as gentle as our master, so we were well off.

I was now beginning to grow handsome; my coat had grown fine and soft, and was bright black. I had one white foot, and a pretty white star on my forehead. I was thought very handsome; my master would not sell me till I was four years old; he said lads ought not to work like men, and colts ought not work like horses till they were quite grown up.

When I was four years old, Squire Gordon came to look at me. He examined my eyes, my mouth, and my legs; he felt them all down; and then I had to walk and trot and gallop before him; he seemed to like me, and said, "When he has been well broken in, he will do very well." My master said he would break me in himself, as he should not like me to be frightened or hurt, and he lost no time about it, for the next day he began.

Everyone may not know what breaking in is, therefore I will describe it. It means to teach a horse to wear a saddle and bridle and to carry on his back a man, woman, or child; to go just the way they wish, and to go quietly. Besides this he has to learn to wear a collar, a crupper, and a breeching, and to stand still while they are put on; then to have a cart or a chaise fixed behind him, so that he cannot walk or trot without dragging it after him; and he must go fast or slow, just as his driver wishes. He must never start at what he sees, nor speak to other horses, nor bite, nor kick, nor have any will of his own; but always do his master's will, even though he may be very tired or hungry; but the worst of all is, when his harness is once on, he may neither jump for joy nor lie down for weariness. So you see this breaking in is a great thing.

I had of course long been used to a halter and a headstall, and to be led about in the field and lanes quietly, but now I was to have a bit and a bridle; my master gave me some oats as usual, and after a good deal of coaxing, he got the bit into my mouth, and the bridle fixed, but it was a nasty thing! Those who have never had a bit in their mouths cannot think how bad it feels; a great piece of cold hard steel as thick as a man's finger to be pushed into your mouth, between your teeth and over your tongue, with the ends coming out of the corners of your mouth, and held fast there by straps over your head, under your throat, round your nose, and under your chin; so that in no way in the world can you get rid of the nasty hard thing; it is very bad! yes, very bad! at least I thought so; but I knew my mother always wore one when she went out, and all horses did when they were grown up; and so, what with the nice oats, and with my master's pats, kind words, and gentle ways, I got to wear my bit and bridle.

Next came the saddle, but that was not half so bad; my master put it on my back very gently, while old Daniel held my head; he then made the girths fast under my body, patting and talking to me all the time; then I had a few oats, then a little leading about, and this he did every day till I began to look for the oats and the saddle. At length, one morning my master got on my back and rode me round the meadow on the soft grass. It certainly did feel queer; but I must say I felt rather proud to carry my master, and as he continued to ride me a little every day I soon became accustomed to it.

The next unpleasant business was putting on the iron shoes; that too was very hard at first. My master went with me to the smith's forge, to see that I was not hurt or got any fright. The blacksmith took my feet in his hand one after the other, and cut away some of the hoof. It did not pain me, so I stood still on three legs till he had done them all. Then he took a piece of iron the shape of my foot, and clapped it on, and drove some nails through the shoe quite into my hoof, so that the shoe was firmly on. My feet felt very stiff and heavy, but in time I got used to it.

And now having got so far, my master went on to break me to harness; there were more new things to wear. First, a stiff heavy collar just on my neck and a bridle with great side-pieces against my eyes called blinkers, and blinkers indeed they were, for I could not see on either side, but only straight in front of me; next there was a small saddle with a nasty stiff strap that went right under my tail; that was the crupper. I hated the crupper—to have my long tail doubled up and poked through that strap was almost as bad as the bit. I never felt more like kicking, but of course I could not kick such a good master, and so in time I got used to everything, and could do my work as well as my mother.

I must not forget to mention one part of my training, which I have always considered a very great advantage. My master sent me for a fortnight to a neighboring farmer's, who had a meadow which was skirted on one side by the railway. Here were some sheep and cows, and I was turned in among them.

I shall never forget the first train that ran by. I was feeding quietly near the pales which separated the meadow from the railway, when I heard a strange sound at a distance, and before I knew whence it came—with a rush and a clatter, and a puffing out of smoke—a long black train of something flew by, and was gone almost before I could draw my breath. I turned and galloped to the farther side of the meadow as fast as I could go, and there I stood snorting with astonishment and fear. In the course of the day many other trains went by, some more slowly; these drew up at the station close by, and sometimes made an awful shriek and groan before they stopped. I thought it very dreadful, but the cows went on eating very quietly, and hardly raised their heads as the great, black, frightful thing came puffing and grinding past.

For the first few days I could not feed in peace; but as I found that this terrible creature never came into the field, or did me any harm, I began to disregard it, and very soon I cared as little about the passing of a train as the cows and sheep did.

Since then I have seen many horses much alarmed and restive at the sight or sound of a steam engine; but thanks to my good master's care, I am as fearless at railway stations as in my own stable. Now if anyone wants to break in a young horse well, that is the way.

My master often drove me in double harness with my mother, because she was steady and could teach me how to go better than a strange horse. She told me the better I behaved, the better I should be treated, and that it was wisest always to do my best to please my master. "But," said she, "there are a great many kinds of men; there are good, thoughtful men like our master that any horse may be proud to serve; but there are bad, cruel men, who never ought to have a horse or dog to call their own. Besides, there are a great many foolish men, vain, ignorant and careless, who never trouble themselves to think; these spoil more horses than all, just for want of sense; they don't mean it, but they do it for all that. I hope you will fall into good hands; but a horse never knows who may buy him, or who may drive him; it is all a chance for us, but still I say, do your best wherever it is, and keep up your good name."

Black Beauty is sold to Squire Gordon and lives with him for three happy years until the mistress of the house becomes ill. He is next sold to Lord W——.

Early in the spring Lord W——and part of his family went up to London, and took York with them. I and Ginger and some other horses were left at home for use, and the head groom was left in charge.

The Lady Harriet, who remained at the Hall, was a great invalid, and never went out in the carriage, and the Lady Anne preferred riding on horseback with her brother or cousins. She was a perfect horsewoman, and as gay and gentle as she was beautiful. She chose me for her horse, and named me "Black Auster." I enjoyed these rides very much in the clear cold air, sometimes with Ginger, sometimes with Lizzie. This Lizzie was a bright bay mare, almost thoroughbred, and a great favorite with the gentlemen, on account of her fine action and lively spirit; but Ginger, who knew more of her than I did, told me she was rather nervous.

There was a gentleman of the name of Blantyre staying at the Hall; he always rode Lizzie, and praised her so much that one day Lady Anne ordered the sidesaddle to be put on her and the other saddle on me. When we came to the door, the gentleman seemed very uneasy.

"How is this?" he said. "Are your tired of your good Black Auster?"

"Oh! no, not at all," she replied, "but I am amiable enough to let you ride him for once, and I will try your charming Lizzie. You must confess that in size and appearance she is far more like a lady's horse than my own favorite."

"Do let me advise you not to mount her," he said. "She is a charming creature, but she is too nervous for a lady. I assure you she is not perfectly safe; let me beg you to have the saddles changed."

Anna Sewell

"My dear cousin," said Lady Anne laughing, "pray do not trouble your good careful head about me. I have been a horsewoman ever since I was a baby, and I have followed the hounds a great many times, though I know you do not approve of ladies hunting; but still that is the fact, and I intend to try this Lizzie that you gentlemen are all so fond of; so please help me to mount like a good friend as you are."

There was no more to be said; he placed her carefully on the saddle, looked to the bit and curb, gave the reins gently into her hand, and then mounted me. Just as we were moving off, a footman came out with a slip of paper and message from the Lady Harriet. "Would they ask this question for her at Dr. Ashley's, and bring the answer?"

The village was about a mile off, and the doctor's house was the last in it. We went along gaily enough till we came to his gate. There was a short drive up to the house between tall evergreens. Blantyre alighted at the gate, and was going to open it for Lady Anne, but she said, "I will wait for you here, and you can hang Auster's rein on the gate."

He looked at her doubtfully. "I will not be five minutes," he said.

"Oh, do not hurry yourself. Lizzie and I shall not run away from you."

He hung my rein on one of the iron spikes, and was soon hidden among the trees. Lizzie was standing quietly by the side of the road a few paces off with her back to me. My young mistress was sitting easily with a loose rein, humming a little song. I listened to my rider's footsteps until they reached the house, and heard him knock at the door. There was a meadow on the opposite side of the road, the gate of which stood open. Just then some cart horses and several young colts came trotting out in a very disorderly manner, while a boy behind was cracking a great whip. The colts were wild and frolicsome, and one of them bolted across the road and blundered up against Lizzie's hind legs;

156

and whether it was the stupid colt, or the loud cracking of the whip, or both together, I cannot say, but she gave a violent kick, and dashed off into a headlong gallop. It was so sudden that Lady Anne was nearly unseated, but she soon recovered herself. I gave a loud, shrill neigh for help; again and again I neighed, pawing the ground impatiently and tossing my head to get the rein loose. I had not long to wait. Blantyre came running to the gate; he looked anxiously about, and just caught sight of the flying figure, now far away on the road. In an instant he sprang to the saddle. I needed no whip, or spur, for I was as eager as my rider; he saw it, and giving me a free rein, and leaning a little forward, we dashed after them.

For about a mile and a half the road ran straight, and then bent to the right, after which it divided into two roads. Long before we came to the bend, she was out of sight. Which way had she turned? A woman was standing at her garden gate, shading her eyes with her hand, and looking eagerly up the road. Scarcely drawing the rein, Blantyre shouted, "Which way?" "To the right," cried the woman, pointing with her hand, and away we went up the right-hand road; then for a moment we caught sight of her; another bend and she was hidden again. Several times we caught glimpses, and then lost them. We scarcely seemed to gain ground upon them at all. An old road mender was standing near a heap of stones—his shovel dropped and his hands raised. As we came near he made a sign to speak. Blantyre drew rein a little. "To the common, to the common, sir; she has turned off there." I knew this common very well; it was for the most part very uneven ground, covered with heather and dark green furze bushes, with here and there a scrubby old thorn tree; there were also open spaces of fine short grass, with anthills and mole turns everywhere; the worst place I ever knew for a headlong gallop.

We had hardly turned on the common, when we caught sight again of the green habit flying on before us. My lady's

hat was gone, and her long brown hair was streaming behind her. Her head and body were thrown back, as if she
were pulling with all her remaining strength, and as if that
strength were nearly exhausted. It was clear that the rough-
ness of the ground had very much lessened Lizzie's speed,
and there seemed a chance that we might overtake her.

While we were on the highroad, Blantyre had given me
my head; but now, with a light hand and a practiced eye, he
guided me over the ground in such a masterly manner that
my pace was scarcely slackened, and we were decidedly
gaining on them.

About halfway across the heath there had been a wide
dike recently cut, and the earth from the cutting was cast up
roughly on the other side. Surely this would stop them! but
no; with scarcely a pause Lizzie took the leap, stumbled
among the rough clods and fell. Blantyre groaned, "Now,
Auster, do your best!" He gave me a steady rein. I gathered
myself well together and with one determined leap cleared
both dike and bank.

Motionless among the heather, with her face to the
earth, lay my poor young mistress. Blantyre kneeled down
and called her name. There was no sound. Gently he turned
her face upward. It was ghastly white, and the eyes were
closed. "Annie, dear Annie, do speak!" but there was no
answer. He unbuttoned her habit, loosened her collar, felt
her hands and wrists, then started up and looked wildly
round him for help.

At no great distance there were two men cutting turf,
who, seeing Lizzie running wild without a rider, had left
their work to catch her.

Blantyre's halloo soon brought them to the spot. The
foremost man seemed much troubled at the sight and asked
what he could do.

"Can you ride?"

"Well, sir, I bean't much of a horseman, but I'd risk my
neck for Lady Anne; she was uncommon good to my wife in
the winter."

"Then mount this horse, my friend; your neck will be quite safe, and ride to the doctor's and ask him to come instantly—then on to the Hall—tell them all that you know, and bid them send me the carriage with Lady Anne's maid and help. I shall stay here."

"All right, sir, I'll do my best, and I pray God the dear young lady may open her eyes soon." Then, seeing the other man, he called out, "Here, Joe, run for some water, and tell my missus to come as quick as she can to the Lady Anne."

He then somehow scrambled into the saddle, and with a "Gee-up" and a clap on my sides with both his legs, he started on his journey, making a little circuit to avoid the dike. He had no whip, which seemed to trouble him, but my pace soon cured that difficulty, and he found the best thing he could do was to stick to the saddle and hold me in, which he did manfully. I shook him as little as I could help, but once or twice on the rough ground he called out, "Steady! Whoa! Steady!" On the highroad we were all right, and at the doctor's and the Hall he did his errand like a good man and true. They asked him in to take a drop of something. "No, no!" he said, "I'll be back to 'em again by a shortcut through the fields, and be there afore the carriage."

There was a great deal of hurry and excitement after the news became known. I was just turned into my box, the saddle and the bridle were taken off, and a cloth thrown over me.

Ginger was saddled and sent off in great haste for Lord George, and I soon heard the carriage roll out of the yard.

It seemed a long time before Ginger came back and before we were left alone; and then she told me all that she had seen.

"I can't tell much," she said. "We went at a gallop nearly all the way, and got there just as the doctor rode up. There was a woman sitting on the ground with the lady's head in her lap. The doctor poured something into her mouth, but all that I heard was, 'She is not dead.' Then I was led off by a man to a little distance. After a while she was taken to the carriage and we came home together. I heard my master say to a gentleman who stopped him to inquire that he hoped no bones were broken, but that she had not spoken yet.''

When Lord George took Ginger for hunting, York shook his head; he said it ought to be a steady hand to train a horse for the first season, and not a random rider like Lord George.

Ginger used to like it very much, but sometimes when she came back I could see that she had been very much strained, and now and then she gave a short cough. She had too much spirit to complain, but I could not help feeling anxious about her.

Two days after the accident, Blantyre paid me a visit. He patted me and praised me very much; he told Lord George that he was sure the horse knew of Annie's danger as well as he did. "I could not have held him in if I would," said he. "She ought never to ride any other horse." I found by their conversation that my young mistress was now out of danger, and would soon be able to ride again. This was good news to me, and I looked forward to a happy life.

———————

Black Beauty is put up for sale after his drunken groom causes him to fall during a dangerous gallop. His knees and appearance are ruined.

No doubt a horse fair is a very amusing place to those who have nothing to lose; at any rate, there is plenty to see.

Long strings of young horses out of the country, fresh from the marshes; and droves of shaggy little Welsh ponies;

and hundreds of cart horses of all sorts, some of them with their long tails braided up, and tied with scarlet cord; and a good many like myself, handsome and highbred, but fallen into the middle class, through some accident or blemish, unsoundness of wind, or some other complaint. There were some splendid animals quite in their prime and fit for anything; they were throwing out their legs and showing off their paces in high style, as they were trotted out with a leading rein, the groom running by the side. But round in the background there were a number of poor things, sadly broken down with hard work, with their knees knuckling over and their hind legs swinging out at every step; and there were some very dejected-looking old horses, with the underlip hanging down and the ears lying back heavily, as if there was no more pleasure in life, and no more hope; there were some so thin you might see all their ribs, and some with old sores on their backs and hips. These were sad sights for a horse to look upon, who knows not but he may come to the same state.

There was a great deal of bargaining, of running up and beating down, and if a horse may speak his mind so far as he understands, I should say, there were more lies told and more trickery at that horse fair than a clever man could give an account of. I was put with two or three other strong, useful-looking horses, and a good many people came to look at us. The gentlemen always turned from me when they saw my broken knees, though the man who had me swore it was only a slip in the stall.

The first thing was to pull my mouth open, then to look at my eyes, then feel all the way down my legs, and give me a hard feel of the skin and flesh, and then try my paces.

It was wonderful what a difference there was in the way these things were done. Some did it in a rough, offhand way, as if one was only a piece of wood; while others would take their hands gently over one's body, with a pat now and then, as much as to say, "By your leave." Of course I

162

judged a good deal of the buyers by their manners to myself.

There was one man, I thought, if he would buy me, I
should be happy. He was not a gentleman, nor yet one of
the loud, flashy sort that called themselves so. He was
rather a small man, but well made and quick in all his mo-
tions. I knew in a moment by the way he handled me that he
was used to horses. He spoke gently, and his gray eye had a
kindly, cheery look in it. It may seem strange to say—but it
is true all the same—that the clean, fresh smell there was
about him made me take to him; no smell of old beer and
tobacco, which I hated, but a fresh smell as if he had come
out of a hayloft. He offered twenty-three pounds for me;
but that was refused, and he walked away. I looked after
him, but he was gone, and a very hard-looking, loud-voiced
man came. I was dreadfully afraid he would have me; but he
walked off. One or two more came who did not mean business.

Then the hard-faced man came back again and offered
twenty-three pounds. A very close bargain was being
driven, for my salesman began to think he should not get all
he asked, and must come down; but just then the gray-eyed
man came back again. I could not help reaching out my
head toward him. He stroked my face kindly.

"Well, old chap," he said, "I think we should suit each
other. I'll give twenty-four for him."

"Say twenty-five and you shall have him."

"Twenty-four ten," said my friend, in a very decided
tone, "and not another sixpence—yes or no?"

"Done," said the salesman, "and you may depend upon
it there's a monstrous deal of quality in that horse, and if
you want him for cab work, he's a bargain."

The money was paid on the spot, and my new master
took my halter, and led me out of the fair to an inn, where
he had a saddle and bridle ready. He gave me a good feed of
oats and stood by while I ate it, talking to himself and

talking to me. Half an hour after, we were on our way to London, through pleasant lanes and country roads, until we came into the great London thoroughfare, on which we traveled steadily, till in the twilight we reached the great city. The gas lamps were already lighted; there were streets to the right, and streets to the left, and streets crossing each other for mile upon mile. I thought we should never come to the end of them. At last, in passing through one, we came to a long cabstand, where my rider called out in a cheery voice, "Good night, Governor!"

"Halloo!" cried a voice. "Have you got a good one?"

"I think so," replied my owner.

"I wish you luck with him."

"Thank ye, Governor," and he rode on. We soon turned up one of the side streets, and about halfway up that we turned into a very narrow street, with rather poor-looking houses on one side, and what seemed to be coach houses and stables on the other.

My owner pulled up at one of the houses and whistled. The door flew open, and a young woman, followed by a little girl and boy, ran out. There was a very lively greeting as my rider dismounted.

"Now then, Harry, my boy, open the gates, and mother will bring us the lantern."

The next minute they were all standing round me in a small stable yard.

"Is he gentle, father?"

"Yes, Dolly, as gentle as your own kitten. Come and pat him."

At once the little hand was patting all over my shoulder without fear. How good it felt!

"Let me get him a bran mash while you rub him down," said the mother.

"Do, Polly, it's just what he wants, and I know you've got a beautiful mash ready for me."

"Sausage dumpling and apple turnover," shouted the

boy, which set them all laughing. I was led into a comfortable, clean-smelling stall, with plenty of dry straw, and after a capital supper I lay down, thinking I was to be happy.

———————

Black Beauty is treated well by Jerry, the London cab driver who bought him at the fair. But when Jerry's health fails Black Beauty is again sold.

I shall never forget my new master; he had black eyes and a hooked nose, his mouth was as full of teeth as a bulldog's, and his voice was as harsh as the grinding of cart wheels over gravel stones. His name was Nicholas Skinner, and I believe he was the same man that poor Seedy Sam drove for.

I have heard men say that seeing is believing; but I should say that feeling is believing; for much as I had seen before, I never knew till now the utter misery of a cab horse's life.

Skinner had a low set of cabs and a low set of drivers; he was hard on the men, and the men were hard on the horses. In this place we had no Sunday rest, and it was in the heat of summer.

Sometimes on a Sunday morning, a party of fast men would hire the cab for the day; four of them inside and another with the driver, and I had to take them ten or fifteen miles out into the country, and back again. Never would any of them get down to walk up a hill, let it be ever so steep, or the day ever so hot—unless, indeed, when the driver was afraid I should not manage it, and sometimes I was so fevered and worn that I could hardly touch my food. How I used to long for the nice bran mash with niter in it that Jerry used to give us on Saturday nights in hot weather that used to cool us down and make us so comfortable. Then we had two nights and a whole day for unbroken rest, and on Monday morning we were as fresh as young horses again; but here, there was no rest, and my driver was just as hard as his master. He had a cruel whip with something so sharp at the end that it sometimes drew blood, and he would even whip me under the belly and flip the lash out at my head. Indignities like these took the heart out of me terribly, but still I did my best and never hung back; for, as poor Ginger said, it was no use; men are the strongest.

My life was now so utterly wretched that I wished I might, like Ginger, drop down dead at my work, and be out of my misery, and one day my wish very nearly came to pass.

I went on the stand at eight in the morning, and had done a good share of work, when we had to take a fare to the railway. A long train was just expected in, so my driver pulled up at the back of some of the outside cabs to take the chance of a return fare. It was a very heavy train, and as all the cabs were soon engaged ours was called for. There was a party of four—a noisy, blustering man with a lady, a little boy, and a young girl, and a great deal of luggage. The lady and the boy got into the cab, and while the man ordered about the luggage, the young girl came and looked at me.

"Papa," she said, "I am sure this poor horse cannot take us and all our luggage so far, he is so very weak and worn out. Do look at him."

"Oh! he's all right, miss," said my driver, "he's strong enough."

The porter, who was pulling about some heavy boxes, suggested to the gentleman, as there was so much luggage, whether he would not take a second cab.

"Can your horse do it, or can't he?" said the blustering man.

"Oh! he can do it all right, sir. Send up the boxes, porter. He could take more than that," and he helped to

166

haul up a box so heavy that I could feel the springs go down.

"Papa, papa, do take a second cab," said the young girl in a beseeching tone. "I am sure we are wrong; I am sure it is very cruel."

"Nonsense, Grace, get in at once, and don't make all this fuss; a pretty thing it would be if a man of business had to examine every cabhorse before he hired it—the man knows his own business of course. There, get in and hold your tongue!"

My gentle friend had to obey, and box after box was dragged up and lodged on the top of the cab, or settled by the side of the driver. At last all was ready, and with his usual jerk at the rein, and slash of the whip, he drove out of the station.

The load was very heavy, and I had had neither food nor rest since the morning; but I did my best, as I always had done, in spite of cruelty and injustice.

I got along fairly till we came to Ludgate Hill, but there the heavy load and my own exhaustion were too much. I was struggling to keep on, goaded by constant chucks of the rein and use of the whip, when, in a single moment—I cannot tell how—my feet slipped from under me, and I fell heavily to the ground on my side. The suddenness and the force with which I fell seemed to beat all the breath out of my body. I lay perfectly still; indeed, I had no power to move, and I thought now I was going to die. I heard a sort of confusion round me, loud, angry voices, and the getting down of the luggage, but it was all like a dream. I thought I heard that sweet, pitiful voice saying, "Oh! that poor horse! it is our fault." Someone came and loosened the throat strap of my bridle, and undid the traces which kept the collar so tight upon me. Someone said, "He's dead, he'll never get up again." Then I could hear the policeman giving orders, but I did not even open my eyes. I could only draw a gasping breath now and then. Some cold water was thrown over my head, and some cordial was poured into my mouth, and something was covered over me. I cannot tell how long I lay there, but I found my life coming back, and a kind-voiced man was patting me and encouraging me to rise. After some more cordial had been given me, and after one or two attempts, I staggered to my feet, and was gently led to some stables which were close by. Here I was put into a well-littered stall, and some warm gruel was brought to me, which I drank thankfully.

In the evening I was sufficiently recovered to be led back to Skinner's stables, where I think they did the best for me they could. In the morning Skinner came with a farrier to look at me. He examined me very closely and said:

"This is a case of overwork more than disease, and if you could give him a run-off for six months he would be able to work again; but now there is not an ounce of strength in him."

"Then he must just go to the dogs," said Skinner. "I have no meadows to nurse sick horses in—he might get well or he might not. That sort of thing don't suit my business; my plan is to work 'em as long as they'll go, and then sell 'em for what they'll fetch, at the knacker's or elsewhere."

"If he was broken-winded," said the farrier, "you had better have him killed out of hand, but he is not. There is a sale of horses coming off in about ten days. If you rest him and feed him up, he may pick up, and you may get more than his skin is worth, at any rate."

Upon this advice, Skinner rather unwillingly, I think, gave orders that I should be well fed and cared for, and the stable man, happily for me, carried out the orders with a much better will than his master had in giving them. Ten days of perfect rest, plenty of good oats, hay, bran mashes, with boiled linseed mixed in them, did more to get up my condition than anything else could have done; those linseed mashes were delicious, and I began to think, after all, it

168

might be better to live than go to the dogs. When the twelfth day after the accident came, I was taken to the sale, a few miles out of London. I felt that any change from my present place must be an improvement, so I held up my head, and hoped for the best.

———

At this sale, of course I found myself in company with the old, broken-down horses—some lame, some broken-winded, some old, and some that I am sure it would have been merciful to shoot.

The buyers and sellers, too, many of them, looked not much better off than the poor beasts they were bargaining about. There were poor old men, trying to get a horse or a pony for a few pounds that might drag about some little wood or coal cart. There were poor men trying to sell a worn-out beast for two or three pounds, rather than have the greater loss of killing him. Some of them looked as if poverty and hard times had hardened them all over; but there were others that I would have willingly used the last of my strength in serving; poor and shabby, but kind and human, with voices that I could trust. There was one tottering old man that took a great fancy to me, and I to him, but I was not strong enough—it was an anxious time! Coming from the better part of the fair, I noticed a man who looked like a gentleman farmer, with a young boy by his side; he had a broad back and round shoulders, a kind, ruddy face, and he wore a broad-brimmed hat. When he came up to me and my companions, he gave a pitiful look round upon us. I saw his eye rest on me; I had still a good mane and tail, which did something for my appearance. I pricked my ears and looked at him.

"There's a horse that has known better days."

"Poor old fellow!" said the boy, "do you think, grand-papa, he was ever a carriage horse?"

"Oh yes! my boy," said the farmer, coming closer, "he might have been anything when he was young; look at his nostrils and his ears, the shape of his neck and shoulders. There's a deal of breeding about that horse." He put out his hand and gave me a kind pat on the neck. I put out my nose in answer to his kindness; the boy stroked my face.

"Poor old fellow! see, grandpapa, how well he understands kindness. Could not you buy him and make him young again, as you did with Ladybird?"

"My dear boy, I can't make all old horses young. Besides, Ladybird was not so very old, as she was run down and badly used."

"Well, grandpapa, I don't believe that this one is old; look at his mane and tail. I wish you would look into his mouth, and then you could tell; though he is so very thin, his eyes are not sunk like some old horses'."

The old gentleman laughed. "Bless the boy! he is as horsey as his old grandfather."

"But do look at his mouth and ask the price; I am sure he would grow young in our meadows."

The man who had brought me for sale now put in his word.

"The young gentleman's a real knowing one, sir. Now the fact is, this 'ere hoss is just pulled down with overwork in the cabs; he's not an old one, and I heerd as how the vetenary should say that a six months' run-off would set him right up, being as how his wind was not broken. I've had the tending of him these ten days past, and a gratefuller, pleasanter animal I never met with, and 'twould be worth a gentleman's while to give a five-pound note for him, and let him have a chance. I'll be bound he'd be worth twenty pounds next spring."

The old gentleman laughed and the little boy looked up eagerly.

"Oh! grandpapa, did you not say the colt sold for five pounds more than you expected? You would not be poorer if you did buy this one."

The farmer slowly felt my legs, which were much swelled and strained; then he looked at my mouth. "Thirteen or fourteen, I should say; just trot him out, will you?"

I arched my poor thin neck, raised my tail a little, and threw out my legs as well as I could, for they were very stiff.

"What is the lowest you will take for him?" said the farmer as I came back.

"Five pounds, sir; the lowest price master set."

"'Tis a speculation," said the old gentleman, shaking his head, but at the same time slowly drawing out his purse, "quite a speculation! Have you any more business here?" he said, counting the sovereigns into his hand.

"No, sir, I can take him to the inn, if you please."

"Do so. I am now going there."

They walked forward, and I was led behind. The boy could hardly control his delight, and the old gentleman seemed to enjoy his pleasure. I had a good feed at the inn, and was then gently ridden home by a servant of my new master's and turned into a large meadow with a shed in one corner of it.

Mr. Thoroughgood, for that was the name of my benefactor, gave orders that I should have hay and oats every night and morning, and the run of the meadow during the day, and "you, Willie," said he, "must take the oversight of him. I give him in charge to you.

The boy was proud of his charge, and undertook it in all seriousness. There was not a day when he did not pay me a visit, sometimes picking me out among the other horses, and giving me a bit of carrot, or something good, or sometimes standing by me while I ate my oats. He always came with kind words and caresses, and of course I grew very fond of him. He called me Old Crony, as I used to come to him in the field and follow him about. Sometimes he brought his grandfather, who always looked closely at my legs.

"This is our point, Willie," he would say. "But he is improving so steadily that I think we shall see a change for the better in the spring."

The perfect rest, the good food, the soft turf, and exercise soon began to tell on my condition and my spirits. I had a good constitution from my mother, and I was never strained when I was young, so that I had a better chance than many horses who have been worked before they came to their full strength.

During the winter my legs improved so much that I began to feel quite young again. The spring came round, and one day in March Mr. Thoroughgood determined that he would try me in the phaeton. I was well pleased, and he and Willie drove me a few miles. My legs were not stiff now, and I did the work with perfect ease.

"He's growing young, Willie. We must give him a little gentle work now, and by midsummer he will be as good as Ladybird. He has a beautiful mouth, and good paces; they can't be better."

"Oh! grandpapa, how glad I am you bought him!"

"So am I, my boy, but he has to thank you more than me; we must now be looking out for a quiet, genteel place for him, where he will be valued."

One day during this summer the groom cleaned and dressed me with such extraordinary care that I thought some new change must be at hand; he trimmed my fetlocks and legs, passed the tarbrush over my hoofs, and even parted my forelock. I think the harness had an extra polish. Willie seemed half anxious, half merry, as he got into the chaise with his grandfather.

"If the ladies take to him," said the old gentleman, "they'll be suited, and he'll be suited. We can but try."

At the distance of a mile or two from the village we came to a pretty, low house, with a lawn and shrubbery at the front and a drive up to the door. Willie rang the bell, and asked if Miss Blomefield or Miss Ellen was at home. Yes, they were. So, while Willie stayed with me, Mr. Thoroughgood went into the house. In about ten minutes he returned, followed by three ladies, one tall, pale lady, wrapped in a white shawl, leaned on a younger lady, with dark eyes and a merry face; the other, a very stately-looking person, was Miss Blomefield. They all came and looked at me and asked questions. The younger lady—that was Miss Ellen—took to me very much; she said she was sure she should like me, I had such a good face. The tall, pale lady said that she should always be nervous in riding behind a horse that had once been down, as I might come down again, and if I did, she should never get over the fright.

"You see, ladies," said Mr. Thoroughgood, "many first-rate horses have had their knees broken through the carelessness of their drivers, without any fault of their own, and from what I see of this horse, I should say, that is his case; but of course I do not wish to influence you. If you incline, you can have him on trial, and then your coachman will see what he thinks of him."

"You have always been such a good adviser to us about our horses," said the stately lady, "that your recommendation would go a long way with me, and if my sister Lavinia sees no objection, we will accept your offer of a trial, with thanks."

It was then arranged that I should be sent for the next day.

Anna Sewell

In the morning a smart-looking young man came for me. At first he looked pleased; but when he saw my knees he said in a disappointed voice:

"I didn't think, sir, you would have recommended my ladies a blemished horse like that."

"Handsome is that handsome does," said my master. "You are only taking him on trial, and I am sure you will do fairly by him, young man, and if he is not as safe as any horse you ever drove, send him back."

I was led home, placed in a comfortable stable, fed, and left to myself. The next day, when my groom was cleaning my face, he said:

"That is just like the star that Black Beauty had; he is much the same height too. I wonder where he is now."

A little further on he came to the place in my neck where I was bled, and where a little knot was left in the skin. He almost started, and began to look me over carefully, talking to himself.

"White star in the forehead, one white foot on the off side, this little knot just in that place"—then looking at the middle of my back—"and as I am alive, there is that little patch of white hair that John used to call 'Beauty's three-penny bit.' It *must* be Black Beauty! Why, Beauty! Beauty! do you know me? little Joe Green that almost killed you?" And he began patting and patting me as if he was quite overjoyed.

I could not say that I remembered him, for now he was a fine grown young fellow, with black whiskers and a man's voice, but I was sure he knew me, and that he was Joe Green, and I was very glad. I put my nose up to him, and tried to say that we were friends. I never saw a man so pleased.

"Give you a fair trial! I should think so indeed! I wonder who the rascal was that broke your knees, my old Beauty! You must have been badly served out somewhere; well,

well, it won't be my fault if you haven't good times of it now. I wish John Manly was here to see you."

In the afternoon I was put into a low park chair and brought to the door. Miss Ellen was going to try me, and Green went with her. I soon found that she was a good driver, and she seemed pleased with my paces. I heard Joe telling her about me, and that he was sure I was Squire Gordon's old Black Beauty.

When we returned, the other sisters came out to hear how I had behaved myself. She told them what she had just heard, and said:

"I shall certainly write to Mrs. Gordon, and tell her that her favorite horse has come to us. How pleased she will be!"

After this I was driven every day for a week or so, and as I appeared to be quite safe, Miss Lavinia at last ventured out in the small close carriage. After this it was quite decided to keep me and call me by my old name of "Black Beauty."

I have now lived in this happy place a whole year. Joe is the best and kindest of grooms. My work is easy and pleasant, and I feel my strength and spirits all coming back again. Mr. Thoroughgood said to Joe the other day:

"In your place he will last till he is twenty years old—perhaps more."

Willie always speaks to me when he can, and treats me as his special friend. My ladies have promised that I shall never be sold, and so I have nothing to fear; and here my story ends. My troubles are all over, and I am at home; and often before I am quite awake, I fancy I am still in the orchard at Birtwick, standing with my old friends under the apple trees.

DANZA

LYNN HALL

(an excerpt)

A sunrise breeze winnowed the grasses, silvered them and exposed the yellow and scarlet wild flowers scattered among them. In the distance, below and beyond the meadow, the Caribbean Sea softened away into the sky. The forest, green on black, rimmed the meadow on three sides and left only the southwest slope open to the distant view.

As though cued by the touch of the sunrise breeze and the golden light that came with it, two figures emerged from the forest on opposite sides of the meadow and progressed slowly toward each other, the boy dawdling in his enjoyment of the moment, and the mare distracted every few steps by one more swatch of grass that had to be eaten.

Their meeting was inevitable; there was no need to hurry to it.

The boy was eleven but small. He was a whip of bamboo clad in old pale jeans and a berry-stained blue shirt; he was huge dark eyes and unruly hair and silences that might have puzzled his family, had they noticed. Paulo Camacho was the second of six and the grandson of Diego Mendez.

The mare also belonged to Diego Mendez. Her designation on the farm records and on her registration was "Number Twenty," palomino mare by Ciervo out of Number Six, foaled April 12, 1951. If the pedigree was

179

valid, her breeding was better than that of the other mares on Diego's farm, and Paulo chose to believe that it was.

"Hi, Twenty. How are you feeling this morning? No baby yet, huh?"

They came together, and the mare rubbed her head hard against Paulo's chest, easing the itch of a fly-bite near her eye. Her hide was a rich copper gold, dappled over her hips and flanks. Her cream-white tail swept, huge and full, to the ground, and her mane was twice as long as the depth of her neck. The forelock that Paulo's fingers straightened and smoothed covered the length of her head. In it, and in the mane and tail, were bits of greenery gathered in the forest as she brushed off her flies against the undergrowth.

Paulo bent low and looked up under the mare. Her udder was stretched and hard and hot under his palm when he touched it. A few drops of milk came, and the mare's ears flattened for an instant at the discomfort of his touch.

"Pretty soon now." Away from his grandfather, Paulo could make his voice sound as though he knew what he was talking about, and the mare accepted his authority.

"Just an easy ride this morning, okay?" He looked into her near-side eye for permission, decided that he saw it there, and led the mare, by a handful of mane toward his mounting rock. Twenty was only fourteen hands tall, no more than average for a Puerto Rican-bred Paso Fino, and during the previous summer Paulo had learned to jump on her from flat ground. But now her barrel was distended with the bulk of her foal and Paulo didn't want to be bouncing and kicking against the unborn baby in his attempts to get above the curve of Twenty's sides.

He mounted instead from the rock, after a quick look back toward the house to be sure no one had followed. To be seen riding the mare, and to be tattled on to Grandfather and face the old man's derision—no, that was a higher price than Paulo wanted to pay, even for the fun of riding Twenty.

As Paulo settled onto the ridge of Twenty's spine the mare lifted her head and tail and moved forward, her eyes on the meadow before her, but her senses all tuned to the boy on her back, to the shift of his negligible weight, the touch of his ankle bones on the skin just back of her elbows and the pull of his hand in her mane. A pleasant lightness filled the mare, as it always did when Paulo rode her. It was this for which she had been bred, she and a hundred generations of her ancestors bred on this tiny island since Columbus brought the first horses to this part of the world. Just a handful of them at first, proud Andalusians and elegant barbs and the small beautiful Spanish jennets with their incredibly smooth four-beat gait. It was these horses and their descendants that had enabled the Spanish to conquer the New World, and when that work was done the horses remained, and in the relative isolation of this island they had evolved into a breed known as the Paso Fino, for the fineness, the smoothness of their paces.

As other breeds were developed to fulfill a need, pulling heavy loads or working cattle or jumping the stone fences of the English countryside, the Paso Fino was bred to give his rider pleasure. The uniquely smooth four-beat gait was retained and improved until it became the smoothest riding of all equine gaits. Beauty and elegance of carriage were prized and retained also, but no breeder sacrificed the cherished purity of gait for details of physical beauty.

Through the generations, the horsemen of Puerto Rico had come to feel the staccato beat of their horses' footfalls in the rhythm of their own heartbeats. The horses had grown to know a sense of completeness only when they carried riders to lift them into that beat, to move with them and balance their heads against their reins, to set the arch of neck and collect the hindquarters so that the movement was perfect and the perfection was as joyful to horse as to rider.

But for the mares this joy was rare. They were female. A

man was less than a man if his mount was less than a stallion, and a mare's value lay in the fame of her sire, or her sons.

And so Paulo Camacho glanced again over his shoulder as he settled into Twenty's stride. Sometimes when he rode her Paulo pretended that she was Bonanza or Bravo or one of the other young stallions in their pens near the house. But a stubborn honesty in him made him dislike the pretense. It wasn't fair to Twenty. And Paulo knew, even if no one else did, that Twenty was the best of his grandfather's horses, mare or no mare.

His ankle bones touched her satin sides. There was an unaccustomed hesitation before she responded. Although her unshod hooves moved noiselessly on the cushions of grass, Paulo could feel her footfalls in a gentle vibration through his seat and up his spine and into his heart. Smoothly as a sailboat in benign waters the mare bore Paulo across the curve of the meadow, her tangled two-foot-long mane wafting around him to brush back his unbuttoned shirt and tickle his stomach.

He giggled. The mare flicked an ear back toward him, and slowed her pace. He touched her sides again with his heels. Momentarily she surged forward, but slowed again almost at once.

"Don't feel like going fast this morning? We'll take it easy. You maybe don't feel too good, carrying that big old foal around inside you, huh?"

As they crested the hill, the other mares appeared, four of them with foals already at their sides, two with bulging bellies and one with neither foal nor expectation. That was Seven, a dark brown mare, bald-faced and blue-eyed and aged beyond use as a brood mare. Paulo looked away from her, knowing that her failure to produce a foal this year meant that she would be sold on the kill market.

Beyond the grazing mares a pole fence marked the boundary of the pasture, and the farm. Paulo managed to take down the top pole without dismounting, and ride Twenty over the bottom pole, but in the end he had to dismount anyway, to replace the upper pole. Sighing, he hauled Twenty by her mane toward a stump and climbed up onto her again.

She was reluctant to leave her pasture.

"Come on, why are you so lazy this morning? Just a little ride, okay? Just up to our place and back, and you can go slow."

By hauling on her mane and leaning dangerously far to the right he managed to turn her and get her started along the track that led into the forest. It had been a logging road once, but was shrunk now to a narrow black-green tunnel into which the sunlight penetrated only in narrow spears that highlighted the flame orange blossoms of the flamboyán trees, the passionflowers, the scarlet and yellow and purple of the parrots and the smaller birds who stitched in and out of sight among the trees. There were satinwoods and mahoganies, survivors of the timber industry, Spanish elm and cedar and candletrees and here and there an old ironwood. Paulo lifted his head and flared his nostrils to the dank, perfumed forest air.

The mare stopped. Paulo urged her on with voice and heels, and she resumed the easy swing of her fino gait. A light sweat was coming under her mane and in her flanks.

The track, which had been rising steadily, crested and dropped and became a footpath too steep for logging trucks ever to have traveled. The mare picked her way down, easing her bulk sideways on the steepest parts.

At the bottom of the slope lay a valley choked with vines and splashed with wildflowers. To Paulo's left a waterfall came down at him, three stories tall but narrow as the span of Paulo's arms. It sheeted and splintered over and around rocks as big as cars and poured itself into a fern-rimmed pool that reflected black and scarlet and green from the forest that overhung it.

For a moment the horse and boy stood broadside to the waterfall and savored the rain of cool water that blew over them. Then, at the prodding of Paulo's heels, Twenty moved on again. She splashed through the stream below the pond, stopping to lower her head for a sip. Up the gentler slope of the far bank they climbed, the mare hanging her head for ballast on the climb, and Paulo aimlessly stripping leaves from the trees they passed.

Again the mare stopped.

"Just a little farther. To our place. You can rest there before we start home." He drummed her sides with his heels and she walked on.

The hair at the base of Twenty's ears began to ridge up in sweaty rims. Paulo saw it and looked down at the mare. Her whole body was wet now, and in Paulo's thighs he could feel a tremor in her body.

It's coming, he thought. *I'm going to see it get born.* The tremor was in him now. He exulted in the knowledge that he and Twenty would be going through the ultimate adventure together.

He dropped to the ground in a sudden surge of tenderness toward the mare, and led the way along the almost invisible path. The mare followed closely, her breath in his hair.

The path emerged in a broad clearing, an oval of brilliant emerald grass too flat, too symmetrical to be natural. Rimming the oval, like teeth around a jaw, stood tablets of stone taller than the mare. Carved on the faces of the stones were ancient gods smiling, scowling, dancing, or glowering omnipotent threats.

As he always did, Paulo stopped at the edge of the oval and stood there with his arm across Twenty's neck, sensing ancient presences.

It was almost five hundred years since the Borinquén Indians had played their deadly games on this ceremonial ball court, games in which the gods, accepting their sacrificial tributes, were the ultimate winners. Five hundred years since the Borinquéns first saw the terrifying figures, half-man, half-horse, that had landed on their island from unimaginable worlds beyond the seas, and galloped and shouted and sometimes separated into two halves—men like themselves and the strange animals that shrilled and pawed the ground.

The Borinquéns were gone now, killed by epidemics that the invaders brought, or by slave labor in the invaders' mines. The ancient paving of the ball court had drifted over with leaves, and the leaves had turned to earth, and grasses and flowers and seedling trees had taken root there. Stone tablets had fallen and their god figures lay face down on the ground in the universal humbling of time.

The ball court was just an oval clearing in the forest now, a safe place for a boy and a mare to have early morning rides away from the ridicule of brothers and grandfather. The old gods were dead long ago, and Paulo felt no fear of them. But sometimes when the wind was just right, or when the sunlight caught a stone-carved face and gave it expression, sometimes when Paulo hit a beautiful solid cracking home run at Pony League practice, then there was a feeling in the back of his mind, almost a stirring of memory that reached far beyond his eleven-year life span.

But this morning Paulo's thoughts were all for the mare. He paused not so much to feel the atmosphere of the place as to look at it from the viewpoint of a mare about to foal. Where would be the best place? If he were Twenty, where would he . . .

With a light shove Twenty walked past Paulo and into the circle of sunlight. Paulo followed. Through the sunny center of the clearing she ambled, and into the black shade beyond. There, near the rim of the ancient court, was a three-sided shelter formed on one side by standing stones and on the two flanking sides by stones that had fallen and become supports for wild tangles of trumpet vines. Here the mare felt sheltered.

Twenty stopped within the natural foaling stall and

stood, head low. The painful shifts and pressures within her ceased to make her uneasy. She was in a good place for her delivery. There were no threats here. There was only the boy, but he was insignificant in comparison to the job ahead of her. She no longer had to carry him nor to respond to his heels; he could be ignored while she did her real work.

Paulo tried to follow Twenty into the small green square, but stopped when the mare glared at him. He backed off a few steps and made himself a seat on the corner of the fallen stone.

The mare's coat was chocolate brown now with her sweat. She grunted and swung her head around to bite at her flanks. She turned and stirred up the long grasses with her feet, and pawed to soften the earth beneath her. She lay down, rose again, and continued her turning, pacing, flank-biting.

Paulo stared at her, his huge dark eyes following every move she made. Sometimes a shiver of uneasiness ran through him when she snapped at her flanks. Was she okay, he wondered? Should he have left her in the pasture? Should he be trying to get her back home or was it too late?

But then Twenty relaxed, and Paulo relaxed, too, and looked around at this place he loved, and thought how perfect it was that Twenty had chosen this time and place and was allowing him to be there. He remembered something his grandfather had said once. "Paulo, I'll tell you something about horses," Diego had said. "They are the only animal I know of that can choose when they'll drop their young. They can hold off going into labor until they want to start it, and that usually means when the humans have left them alone. They want privacy, even the gentlest pet horses."

Paulo felt the honor of the tribute Twenty was paying him.

Twenty jerked her head up and stared, wild-eyed, as amniotic water streamed down her hind legs. Paulo sat up, tensed for action. But nothing more happened, and Twenty relaxed again.

Paulo stretched out on his side, among the trumpet vines that cushioned the slab of rock. Their bright orange flowers brushed his elbow and his face. Staring at Twenty, Paulo's eyes went out of focus and he remembered the beginning of their friendship.

It was five years ago. The horses had just arrived—six mares and a stallion trucked up from Ponce one hot July afternoon. Those seven horses were Diego's dream; Paulo had not been too young to feel the impact of his grandfather's emotions as the horses clattered down the ramp. For as long as Paulo could remember, Diego had talked about horses, horses he had owned or known or ridden in the past, horses he wanted to breed. But there had been no money to buy horses. Diego had had only seasonal work in the sugar cane fields and the cane crops weren't good, this high up the mountains. There had been road construction jobs sometimes, and truck driving for the sugar central when Diego's back went bad and he could no longer do the grueling field work at cane harvest. There had been pigs and chickens and the garden to feed the family, but no extra money for buying fine horses.

Then suddenly it had come. A four-acre piece of land on Phosphorescent Bay near La Parguera, a tiny farm Diego had inherited from his mother, was sold to a rich American company for a tourist hotel. The price they paid for the land wasn't big, but it was enough to buy one fine stallion and a handful of comparatively inexpensive brood mares.

The mares were examined when they arrived, and gloated over and even petted by the children. But Diego's love was all for the stallion. Paulo stood aside and watched, and wondered at the intensity of his grandfather's absorption with the stallion.

Bonanza was magnificent, Paulo had to admit. He was a

187

dark mahogany bay like fine old polished wood. He had two low white stockings on his hind feet, just to his pasterns, and a round white star on his forehead, which was usually hidden beneath the fall of forelock that covered his face. His mane hung to his elbow, and his tail was a full proud plume that brushed the ground even when he lifted it in excitement. His head was small and fine and straight-planed, his tiny muzzle dominated by flaring nostrils.

Even in the somewhat dilapidated farmyard, against a backdrop of tin-roofed sheds and bamboo-fenced corrals, Bonanza carried himself with tightly tucked head and arched neck, his clean fine legs moving in a quick-rhythmed dance.

The mares were turned out in their new pasture, and Bonanza was saddled. Paulo watched from a little distance while Diego pulled himself, somewhat stiffly, up onto Bonanza's back. They moved away through the dust of the farmyard, Bonanza snorting and shying at the rooster, at the sow squealing in her pen, at the younger children darting and yelling. But the old man sat erect, his thick body balanced over the horse's center of gravity, his white hair moving slightly around his ears. His square face was oddly blank, not from absence of emotion but from excess. As Bonanza turned and came back past Paulo, the boy was startled to see tears shining in Diego's eyes. Paulo looked away.

For several minutes the proud old man and the gleaming stallion circled the yard. Then finally they came to a stand-still near Res. Res was nine, three years older than Paulo and superior in every way that counted. He was utterly fearless. He would walk in with the sow and her baby pigs, and taunt Paulo for staying on the fence. He was a better ball player, and he had curly hair and the kind of twinkly-eyed face that made older people say silly things about what a charmer he was going to be when he got older.

Diego dismounted and motioned to Res. The boy came

forward, grinning, and stepped up into the stirrup with a
boost in the seat from Diego. "Take him around," the old
man said. "See what it feels like to be a man."

Bonanza bore his small rider away across the glaring
expanse of dust. His hooves pattered their quick-beat
rhythm as he carried his small rider in a smooth flow above
the ground. Res grinned, and something in Paulo went sour.

The rooster ignored the approach of the horse until
Bonanza was on top of him, then with a squawk and a great
beating of wings he rose under Bonanza's belly. The horse,
startled, half reared and wheeled. Paulo's heart leaped, but
Res laughed, regained his shaken balance, and sent
Bonanza in pursuit of the fleeing rooster.

When Res brought the horse back Diego turned to
Paulo. "Ride?"

Paulo hung back. He would have done almost anything
to make his grandfather look at him with the same kind of
pride that Res could engender on that big square face. Almost anything, but the horse was so huge, up close, so
snorty, so nervous and quick in his movements.

Res said, "Come on, baby. You can ride up behind me.
I'll steer him. All you have to do is hang on."

"But what if you fall off?" Paulo demanded. Res and
Grandfather laughed, but then Grandfather started showing
Res how to hold the reins in his hands, and they forgot
about Paulo.

Paulo slipped around the corner of the house and started
running, around the new corrals and out into the meadow
where he could be alone. He hated Res for being better than
he was, and he hated Diego for witnessing his failure and
expecting no better from little baby Paulo. He even almost
hated Bonanza.

But there were the mares. He walked out among them
and felt better, seeing that they were as timid with him as he
had been with Bonanza. They needed his reassurance that
he wouldn't hurt them, and he needed to feel that something

in this world respected him enough to fear him a little.

Most of the mares gently avoided him, allowing him to come within a few feet and then moving away a step at a time, grazing as they went. But one of them didn't evade him.

She was the copper-colored one with the long white mane and tail and the huge soft dark eyes. When Paulo reached toward her face she stood still and half closed her eyes as though that small brown hand felt good against her face bones. As long as he was touching her, the mare stood still. If he removed his hand she shifted and reached for a bite of grass, but at his touch, on her leg or her ribs or down her tail, she stood still again.

Her back was up there above Paulo's head. It was as high as Bonanza's but it seemed a friendly back. A safe place to sit. Maybe even a fun place.

When the mare's grazing took her near an outcropping of rock Paulo climbed up, sucked in his breath in a quick prayer, and flung himself across her back. She lifted her head but didn't move away. By the time he had thrashed and twisted and gotten himself astride, the mare was grazing again, twitching her skin against the flies and lashing her long tail around and over Paulo's legs.

"I can ride, too," the boy cried silently. "See, Grandfather, I can ride, too."

He leaned down and wrapped his arms around the mare's neck, and bawled.

Twenty lowered herself to the grass, grunting. Paulo tensed, but held himself still. This was no time to distract her with reminders of his presence.

She lifted her tail and stretched her legs taut against the force inside her. She felt herself breaking open. Her muscles surged in a mighty squeeze.

A bubble of fluid ballooned out beneath her tail and within it were two hooves, one slightly ahead of the other.

190

Another mighty contraction forced the bubble farther out. Cradled along the forelegs was a head, its outline just suggested to Paulo, through the membrane and the fluid that surrounded it.

For several minutes the mare rested and breathed and gathered her strength. Then came a tremendous contraction and the bulky mass of the foal's shoulders emerged.

Paulo's ears were ringing and he felt suddenly dizzy.

Twenty grunted and pushed, and the foal shot out onto the grass, where it lay wet and covered with the clinging birth sac. The sac was ruptured now, and the fluid that had cushioned and fed the foal for eleven months was drained away into the ground where, centuries ago, the blood of sacrificial offerings had soaked away to nourish the roots of the flowers.

The foal stirred and lifted its head in a wobbly gesture. A foreleg stirred and braced against the earth, but then relaxed for a gathering of strength.

After a few minutes Twenty shifted and scrambled to her feet, tearing the cord that still connected her to her foal. She turned and began to nuzzle and lick the baby. Its head weaved and wobbled under her shoving muzzle, and after a while it tried to struggle to its feet. It got halfway up, almost far enough for Paulo to see whether it was a filly or a stud colt. Then it sank again for another rest.

"Be a stud colt," Paulo breathed. Until that moment he hadn't cared much whether it was a stud or a filly, but now that he had witnessed the birth—something that he had never done before—Paulo felt a bursting kinship with this foal. It was as though Twenty was giving him this foal of hers, as though she knew that Paulo was big enough and a good enough rider that he no longer needed to ride mares in the privacy of the forest. He was ready for a stallion now.

Paulo knew, too, that if it was a filly it would be sold to the first buyer who came along after weaning time. But a stud colt out of Twenty, that would be a horse Grandfather would value. Bravo was a son of Twenty and Bonanza, and Bravo was a source of shining pride to Diego. If this one was a stud colt he wouldn't be sold. And he would be Paulo's special horse, as Bravo was Res's.

Paulo sucked in his breath as the foal made one more thrashing attempt to rise, and succeeded. It stood weaving atop its outpropped legs. Paulo slid down from his stone and approached. The foal felt damp and woolly under his palm. He lifted its tail and looked.

Stud colt!

He grinned till his face ached, and wrapped his arms around the foal's neck. It leaned against him for an instant, until Twenty pushed Paulo's arm away with her muzzle.

Paulo backed away then and watched while the foal shuffled and bumped toward the mare's udder. As his coat dried he became an odd shade of brown, almost maroon. His legs were a dull gray-cream, his mane and tail black. There was no white on him anywhere.

Through the long morning hours and into the afternoon Paulo waited and watched. He felt the pull of people at home wondering where he was, and Saturday chores piling up. But this was more important.

Finally Twenty seemed rested enough for the walk home, and the foal was maneuvering his legs reasonably well. Paulo took the mare by the mane and began the slow walk back across the clearing, down the hill, and across the stream.

The foal followed well enough until they came to the stream. Twenty whickered for him to follow, and he tried, but he couldn't lift his feet high enough off the ground to negotiate the slight drop into the water.

Paulo tried to wrap his arms around the foal and lift him, but the colt was too heavy. Paulo got behind and pushed, and with a squeal and a splash the foal was in the water. It came only halfway to his knees. He made a scrambling lunge and came out the other side and pressed close to the mare for reassurance.

192

Lynn Hall

Up the far slope they moved, and onto the old timber road. Paulo followed behind, now that Twenty was heading for home and needed no encouragement.

On the flat open track the mare increased her speed. Suddenly the foal lifted himself from his shuffling walk and swung into the beautiful rhythmic gait that is the birthright of every Paso Fino foal.

Like a Spanish dancer, Paulo thought. From his memory of Grandfather's list of names for future foals, Paulo focused on one name.

Danza.